"Damnation, Woman!"

Jess swore. "What are you doing down here, anyway?"

"Well, excuse me, Mr. Hubbard," Terry sputtered. "But I've got as much right to be in this kitchen as you do!"

"That's a matter of opinion," he growled as he caught sight of the feathery pink puffs peeking out from beneath her nightgown. "What the devil do you think this is?" he asked, unable to stop his heated gaze from ascending from her fancy slippers to her long legs, womanly hips and full breasts outlined in shimmering, hot-pink silk. "A ranch house or a bordello?"

"What!"

"That getup sure doesn't leave much to the imagination. Not that I mind, of course," he drawled. "You really can't blame me for wondering if you've forgotten where you are."

"I know exactly where I am, Mr. Hubbard, and I also know exactly what kind of man I'm with...a low-down, conniving—"

"If that's how you feel," he said, cutting her off, "you must really be desperate for a man. Or does your body perk up like that for every lowlife you happen to encounter?"

Dear Reader:

Sensuous, emotional, compelling . . . these are all words that describe Silhouette Desire. If this is your first Desire novel, let me extend an invitation for you to revel in the pleasure of a tantalizing, fulfilling love story. If you're a regular reader, you already know that you're in for a treat!

A Silhouette Desire can encompass many varying moods and tones. The story can be deeply moving and dramatic, or charming and lighthearted. But no matter what, each and every Silhouette Desire is a terrific romance written by and for today's woman.

April is a special month here at Silhouette Desire. First, there's *Warrior,* one of Elizabeth Lowell's books in the *Western Lovers* series. And don't miss *The Drifter* by Joyce Thies, April's *Man of the Month,* which is sure to delight you.

Paula Detmer Riggs makes her Silhouette Desire debut with *Rough Passage,* an exciting story of trust and love. Rounding out April are wonderful stories by Laura Leone, Donna Carlisle and Jessica Barkley. There's something for everyone, every mood, every taste.

So give in to Desire . . . you'll be glad you did.

All the best,

Lucia Macro
Senior Editor

JOYCE
THIES

THE DRIFTER

SILHOUETTE *Desire*®

Published by Silhouette Books New York

America's Publisher of Contemporary Romance

SILHOUETTE BOOKS
300 East 42nd St., New York, N.Y. 10017

THE DRIFTER

ISBN: 0-373-05636-2

First Silhouette Books printing April 1991

Books by Joyce Thies

Silhouette Desire

Territorial Rights #147
Spellbound #348
False Pretenses #359
The Primrose Path #378
†*Moon of the Raven* #432
†*Reach for the Moon* #444
†*Gypsy Moon* #456
Mountain Man #511
King of the Mountain #563
The Drifter #636

*written as Melissa Scott

†Rising Moon series

JOYCE THIES

has been reading and writing romances since her teens but had to wait ten years before one was published. Since then she has authored or coauthored over twenty contemporary and historical novels. Readers might recognize her as the Joyce half of Janet Joyce. She wrote her first Silhouette Desire, *Territorial Rights,* as Melissa Scott, but is now writing under her own name.

She met her husband in college, and it was love at first sight. Joyce believes that out of sharing comes growth for both partners. She says, ''Because of the loving man in my life, I've become everything I've ever wanted to be—wife, mother and writer. With each book I write, I imagine another woman lucky enough to have it all.''

Prologue

By the age of eighteen, Jesse Hubbard knew exactly which floorboards to avoid when he sneaked out of the house at night. Sometimes he'd gone out to the grape arbor for a hot necking session with his girlfriend Lottie Jean Hollister. Other times he'd met his buddies behind the Golden Antler tavern, and they'd slogged down a few beers before getting up a game of poker. As far as he knew, none of the three women who had raised him had ever been aware of his late-night comings and goings.

Tonight, however, was a different story. The instant he stepped outside onto the shadowed front porch, his Great-Aunt Ophelia, an eagle-eyed female in her midsixties, swooped out at him from the darkness. The long, cotton nightgown billowing around her reed-thin body reminded Jesse of the flapping wings on a night-preying hawk right before the kill, and the arthritic fingers biting into the skin of his left arm felt very much like talons. Although he was almost a foot taller and far stronger than his elderly aunt, Jesse made no attempt to break out of her hold.

"Plannin' to sneak off like some thief in the night, were you, Jesse Ray?" Ophelia demanded tartly, dropping his arm in disgust and pointing to the knapsack on his back. "I shure figured we raised you up to show more courage than that."

With a resigned sigh, Jesse pushed back the stubborn lock of blond hair that was always falling down over his forehead. Since he hadn't told another soul about his plans, he couldn't figure out how his aunt had learned about them, but there was no doubt in his mind that she knew. At least, she knew part of it. Unfortunately for him, she and her sisters had taught him never to lie.

"Maybe my leavin' this way is cowardly, Aunt Ophelia," he admitted, shrugging his broad shoulders uncomfortably. "But you know I'm not much for goodbyes. Besides, if I cut out in the daylight, Glory will put up such a fuss that the boys will try and stop me. I figured this way was the best for all of us."

The anger died out of the old woman's face just as the moon came out from behind the clouds to light her white hair like a halo. "You figured right there, Jesse," she agreed, her thin lips curved upward in a reluctant smile. "Now how on this earth would your brothers and sister let you go without fightin' you every step of the way. I still cain't say I like this idea of your'n, but if you've gotta go, I reckon this way is best.''

Grateful for her understanding, Jesse tried to explain his motives for leaving home, aware that he owed her that much. To be honest, he owed her and his Aunts Winnie and Carrie more than he could ever repay. Since the death of his parents twelve years before, they had sacrificed everything they had for his welfare and that of his three brothers and sister.

"There's no money for college, and you know I'm not cut out to work in the mill. And times being what they are, that's the only place hiring," he explained. "There's no future for me in Hillsboro, not with..." His voice trailed off, pride preventing him from voicing his main reason for leaving the small, West Virginian town and the family who loved him.

"Not with Lottie Jean Hollister breakin' your heart by runnin' off with that flashy bank clerk from Radford." Ophelia finished his sentence for him, the sympathy in her tone making Jesse's stomach churn. Was there anything the blamed woman didn't know about his private business? he wondered indignantly.

Before Jesse bothered to deny it, Ophelia went on, "S'pect Lottie figured her prospects were better with him than with you, but that only goes to show what little sense that gal has. You may not believe it now, son, but she twern't right for you. If she were, she would've seen what most folks know 'bout you already. For all your rebellious ways, Jesse Ray Hubbard, you're 'bout as bright as they come and it's right certain you're goin' to make somethin' of yourself someday.''

"But not in this town," Jesse insisted grimly, wishing the moon would go back behind the clouds and hide his flushed face. He hated thinking about Lottie's betrayal, but the thought that anyone else knew how badly she'd humiliated him doubled his pain. "There's nothing for me here."

"Not a whole lot here for any of us. It's just that some of us are more willin' than others to make do," Ophelia declared in her usual practical manner as she reached down into the wide, deep pocket of her nightgown. A moment later she lifted Jesse's hand and pressed something into his palm.

"I cain't stop you from goin'," she allowed, eyes misted in a rare show of emotion. "But I can help you to make your way in the world. Use this for luck unless you get in real desperate straits. Do that and it will serve you well."

After a dramatic pause, she warned in an ominous tone, "But mark my words, boy, if you just fritter this away on nonsense, you'll wish I never gave it to you."

Jesse stared down at the twenty-dollar gold piece in his hand, eyes widening in astonishment as a shaft of moonlight highlighted the mint date. Even without the additional value placed on the coin by its age, it was more money than he or anyone else in the family had ever possessed at one time. "Where in tarnation did you get this, Aunt Ophelia?"

His aunt gave a delighted laugh, and since Jesse couldn't recall a single occasion when he'd heard the most taciturn of his three great-aunts laugh in pure enjoyment like that, his astonishment doubled. Still chuckling, the woman sat down on the porch swing and motioned for him to join her.

As soon as he'd folded his lean, lanky body onto the lumpy seat, she declared, "Now the story behind that coin takes a fair deal of tellin' for there's the good and the bad of using blood money."

"Blood money!"

With a wicked gleam in her eyes, Ophelia teased, "Yes indeed, but seeing's how you're so anxious to leave us, Jesse Ray, maybe you cain't stay to hear all about the legacy my Great-Grandmother Cornelia Hubbard left to her kin."

The night was still young, but even if it hadn't been, Jesse's answer would've been the same. "I can stay for a spell, Aunt Ophelia," he replied, removing his knapsack so he could lean back more comfortably beside her. "Sunrise is a long way off yet."

Much more aware of the swift passage of time than a young man of his age could ever be, Ophelia merely nodded, her expression sad as she set the swing into motion. Then, with her crackling voice conveying a mixture of mystery and reverence, she passed on the secret of the Hubbard fortune to the next generation.

One

The sun had been up for well over an hour, but instead of being outside pitching hay to the hungry stock milling around in the feedlot, Jess was still inside the white clapboard ranch house, seated at the kitchen table. Tanned forearms resting on either side of his empty plate, he stared down at the red and white checkered pattern on the spattered oilcloth. With tight-lipped deliberation, he counted the red squares, then the white ones. He wasn't aware that his silent count was accompanied by the clenching and unclenching of his fists, but the bearded, gray-haired man seated across from him was acutely aware of it.

The big oak grandfather clock in the front room ticked several more times before Jess regained enough calm to talk. "Why, Sam? Why in hell would you sell me out like this?"

Samuel Lawson shifted uneasily in his hard, straight-backed chair, thanking his lucky stars that he was long past his prime and the two-fisted man in the opposite chair was still in his early thirties. Yes indeedy, it was lucky for him that he was wearing the protective cloak of old age, for if he'd been any younger, Sam knew that Jess Hubbard's fists would be doing most of his talking this morning.

"I surely wish you wouldn't see it that way, Partner." Sam said, flinching apprehensively when Jess brought up his hand to swipe at the stubborn lock of gold hair that habitually fell down over his forehead.

Noting the older man's defensive movement, Jess smiled, but he knew the slight upward curve of his lips conveyed little humor to Sam. "How else should I see it, *Partner?*"

"All I did was sell half of my share of the ranch to my granddaughter," Sam said nervously, understanding now why young children hid behind their mama's skirts when they saw this man walking down Main Street. "Since you own a full fifty percent of the Triple L, why should you care if my Terry owns a mere quarter?"

"Why should I care!" Jess exclaimed in furious disbelief, picturing Sam's face beneath his clenched fist as he pounded it on the table. "Why should I care!"

Sensing that his outraged partner had many more reasons to care than he'd ever previously suspected, Sam insisted plaintively, "C'mon Jess. Can't you understand why I done it? Terry's all I got . . . the last of the Lawsons. Is it so wrong for me to want my only kin close by?''

Having lived with this ornery, old coot for the past year, Jess was astonished by the sentimental outburst. From the very beginning of their association, Sam had made it clear that he considered himself as tough as old boot leather. Up until this morning, Jess had never heard the man admit to needing anything or anybody, even on those days when his arthritis was so bad that he could barely make it out of bed. So what had prompted this drastic change of heart?

Struck by a suspicion that turned his blood cold, Jess demanded, "Have you been feeling poorly lately?"

Sam was taken aback by the question, but he managed to conceal his surprise. Jess might still be angry enough to spit tacks, but just for a second, there had been a slight softening in his tone. A man didn't last for three-quarters of a century without picking up a few survival skills along the way, and Sam Lawson was definitely a survivor. Course he realized that making a ploy like this work would call for some mighty fine acting on his part, but considering how poorly their discussion had gone up until now, Sam was more than willing to give playacting a try.

"At my age, a man has his good days and his bad days," he replied gruffly, careful not to reveal any unnatural weakness in his voice, knowing Jess was too smart to buy such an obvious gambit.

"More bad than good?"

Sam shrugged as if he hadn't thought much about it, then thrust out his chin at a belligerent angle. "I ain't complaining," he growled, allowing his gnarled fingers to tremble only slightly as he reached for his coffee cup.

Jess noted the tremble, and although he still felt betrayed, his rage slowly began to subside. One glance at that stubbornly set chin told Jess that the proud older man didn't want to talk about his declining health and there was no use in asking him any further questions about it. Sam Lawson wouldn't complain even if death came knocking at the door, and Jess had to admire that kind of fortitude.

Unfortunately the respect he felt for the man often short-circuited Jess's annoyance whenever Sam championed some harebrained scheme. This time, however, his wily old partner hadn't just gone behind his back to purchase a dozen beefalo or some other equally outrageous action. This time, Sam had royally screwed up the works.

"Don't you think I had a right to know about this damned fool plan of yours before you put it into action?" Jess demanded, spearing Sam with a look that could've melted steel.

Deciding that in this particular instance, honesty might very well be the best policy, Sam admitted, "If I'd told you, you would've put the kibosh on the idea right pronto."

"You've got that right."

"Even though we're always short on ready cash and Terry made me a generous offer," Sam complained.

"Even so."

"And you'd never even consider taking on a female partner."

"Running a ranch this size is hard enough work for a man," Jess agreed, then reminded bluntly. "And you share that opinion."

"But Terry's not just any woman, she's my granddaughter," Sam said, as if that should explain everything.

"A granddaughter who loves this place so much that she left the instant she turned eighteen?" Jess demanded, and when Sam made no attempt to dispute that allegation, he growled, "C'mon, old man, this deal makes absolutely no sense and you know it."

Instead of responding to that possibility, Sam accused, "See? I could've talked myself blue in the face without convincing you that I did the right thing."

"Well, you've got me there," Jess retorted sarcastically.

Sam threw up his hands, plainly unwilling to continue their debate. "Then all I can say is what's done is done."

Jess shook his head, resigned to Sam's fatalistic philosophy, if not the situation. "What's done is done," he agreed, but to keep Sam from assuming that he'd meekly accepted his fate, he quickly added. "But it doesn't necessarily have to stay done."

Sam was deaf to that warning. "You'll like Terry," he insisted, smiling at Jess through his grizzled, grey beard. "She's a real good egg."

"And you know how I feel about eggs, damn you," Jess retorted snidely, the heels of his boots hitting the warped linoleum floor with a sharp crack as he dropped his feet off the step stool and stood up from the table. The incorrigible old man just didn't know when to quit, but this time, Sam was going to find out that Jess could be every bit as stubborn. For once, he decided, the old hornswoggler was not going to have everything his own way.

Sam could sugarcoat the facts about his grand-daughter all he wanted, but Jess still refused to swallow them. Even if Terry Lawson Brubacker did turn out to be the sweet, loving angel that Sam purported her to be, the Triple L ranch was a long way from heaven and no place for her...or any other woman. For the life of him, Jess couldn't figure out why any female would want a share of so many problems, but then he glanced over at Sam and realized that since the old man had kept him in the dark, he wouldn't be above doing the same with his granddaughter. The poor woman probably had no idea what kind of trouble she was walking into or what kind of man she was going to be dealing with.

Blue eyes narrowed with suspicion, Jess rasped, "I hope you told her that owning a quarter share of this place doesn't entitle her to an opinion on how it's going to be run."

As he searched for a reply that wouldn't land him in even hotter water, Sam grabbed for a piece of cold toast and dunked it into his coffee. "Don't worry, Jess," he finally answered lightly. "Terry's got a pretty good head on her shoulders."

Jess's retort was instant. "Meaning you neglected to tell her that I call all the shots!"

Sam rubbed his stubbled chin, striving for an ab-sentminded expression. "Cain't rightly say that I did or I didn't."

"Great! That's just great!" Back ramrod straight, Jess marched over to the grease-spattered stove and picked up the sooty metal pot. In desperate need of some nonviolent means to ease his frustration, he poured himself a cup of thick, black coffee, but after only one sip, he leaned over the sink and spit out the evil tasting brew. "Hell!"

"Terry makes a great cup of coffee," Sam assured him, then tacked on for good measure. "And she can cook just as fine as any French chef."

"Swell," Jess muttered, taking an almost vicious swipe at the burnished blond lock that swept his forehead. "That's really what we need on this place. A fancy pants city woman who thinks some prissy soufflés and crepes will fill a working man's stomach."

Having deliberately insulted Sam's beloved only grandchild, Jess was expecting a far different comeback than the one he got.

"Mmm," Sam murmured, smacking his lips as he gingerly pulled his work gloves on over the arthritic joints of his fingers. "I never had me none of those Frenchy dishes. Them crepes taste any good?"

When that question was greeted with nothing but a stony silence, Sam noted indignantly, "Well, it's for certain, whatever Terry cooks will be better than anything you or I can fix."

Jess had no argument with the man there, which only meant that he would have to attack the problem from a different angle. Maybe this rich, time-on-her-hands divorcée who hailed from some swanky suburb in Chicago had convinced her grandfather that she'd developed a sudden yearning for life in the wide open spaces, but Jess didn't buy that malarkey for a second. That kind of woman wanted something besides the simple life, and he was damned well going to find out what it was before she moved in on them lock, stock, and barrel.

"If that woman thinks so much of you and this ranch, how come she's never been out here before?" Jess inquired, grabbing one side of Sam's denim jacket and holding it up so the older man could push his stiff arm through the sleeve. "I've been living here for almost a year, and up until today, I didn't even know you had a granddaughter."

"Terry was born and raised on this ranch, but she married a man who wanted to be a big-time lawyer. From the first, Doug Brubacker had his sights set on the city," Sam informed him as the two men walked out of the house together and ambled side by side toward the stock pens. "What with goin' through the divorce and all, she hadn't been able to come out in a while, but she's been writing me every chance she gets."

Jess considered that telling comment for a moment, plagued by an inkling that frayed his already ragged temper. "And I suppose you write her back just as often?"

"Sure do."

"Then I take it that you happened to mention me, even if you did leave out the part about me running the show?"

"Your name came up," Sam agreed.

"More than my name," Jess corrected tersely. "In actual fact, you told her every last thing you know about me."

"Not much to tell there," Sam retorted, but the brief reply told Jess plenty.

"Jeezus!" he swore as the truth dawned on him. "I suppose you let her think that some smooth-talking cowboy moved in on you, didn't you?"

Sam shrugged his thin shoulders dismissively, then winced at the pain it caused in his spine. "Had to do something to save those boys before it's too late. Right up to settlement day, Doug Brubacker had them taking tennis lessons and playing the violin. Can you believe it?"

Jess stopped in midstride. "Boys! What boys?"

"Didn't I tell ya?" Sam inquired innocently, though he wisely kept on walking. "Terry's got two sons. Chadwick's 'bout seven, and Charlton's two years younger."

"Chadwick and Charlton!"

"That ought to tell ya plenty about Douglas Winston Brubacker III," Sam growled. "What kind of man would name his sons Chadwick and Charlton? Well, out here they won't be goin' by them namby-pamby names. Chad and Chuck, that's what I call 'em."

"Chadwick and Charlton," Jess groaned, feeling a sinking sensation deep down in his gut. "Teresa, Chadwick, and Charlton. My God, Sam, what did I ever do to deserve this?"

"It's Terry, Chad, and Chuck," Sam corrected, but thought better of responding to that last loaded question even though he had a ready answer. Hiding a smug smile beneath the broad brim of his battered Stetson, he waited for Jess to work the rusty metal hinge on the nearest corral. Of course, he was more than capable of completing the simple task himself, but since Jess had come there was no need to put his aching fingers through the torture. Yes indeedy, since Jess had come, he'd started breathing a whole lot easier, and once Terry arrived he'd be even more content.

Irked by the complacent expression on his partner's face, Jess didn't utter another word until he'd shouldered a bale of hay and stalked to the small feedlot that held a half-dozen or so injured yearlings. Dropping the bale on the ground, he reached into the back pocket of his jeans for the metal cutter. "Okay, Sam. Let's hear the rest of the details," he prompted wearily. "When can I expect to meet this highfalutin' trio?"

As was their custom, Sam stood by warming his hands in his pockets while Jess cut the metal band off the bale and picked up a pitchfork. "Spect they'll be here 'round sunset."

"Sunset," Jess repeated through gritted teeth, tempted to pitch a scrawny old man into the feedlot right along with the hay. "Sunset tonight."

Hearing that calm, deadly tone, Sam was reminded of a famous gunslinger he'd once seen in the movies naming the hour for an upcoming showdown. That image raised the short hairs on the back of his neck and also made him wonder if he hadn't jumped the gun here somewhat himself. Maybe he didn't know Jess Hubbard quite as well as he thought.

"Now you'll be nice to her, son, won't ya?" he pleaded gruffly. "She's been through a real hard time with Douglas this past year, and if I'm any judge of character, a few years before that, too."

Jess's silvery blue eyes were as frigid as Sam had ever seen them, and he couldn't help but shiver when he looked into them.

"If you were any judge of character, old man," Jess replied, giving the hay bale another vicious thrust with his pitchfork, "you'd renege on your deal and advise her not to come."

It was a three-hour drive from the airport in Butte to the Triple L ranch, but with two restless, little boys whining and fighting in the back seat of the rental car, it seemed to Terry that the drive was taking several hours longer. Adding to her irritability was the knowledge that she was about to come face-to-face with the no-account drifter who had swindled her sweet, gullible grandfather out of half of his property. Thankfully the judge who'd heard her divorce case had staunchly believed in the sanctity of the marriage bed and had provided her with the financial means to take the first legal step in protecting her sons' future interests.

Unlike Grandpa Sam, she wasn't satisfied with being only part owner of the ranch. The Triple L had been owned by her family for six generations, and no stranger was going to walk in and make off with her children's rightful heritage. Not if she had anything to say about it, which she certainly did, now that her name also appeared on the deed.

It was difficult for Terry to block out the criminal thoughts she harbored against Jesse Hubbard, and almost impossible to tune out the horrific noise her sons were making, but the closer she got to her childhood home, the easier it was to concentrate on the glorious scenery surrounding them. It was springtime, her favorite time of year in the mountains, and her memories of this beautiful section of Montana hadn't been the least diminished by her long absence.

The wildflowers that grew up by the edge of the highway were still as colorful as the last time she'd driven down this winding road, and the pungent scents of timothy, sage, broom mustard, and yellow sweet clover that drifted through the open windows of the car were still as fragrant as any Arabian spice market. Circumstances had prevented her from visiting the ranch in almost two years, but she experienced the same kind of excitement and eager anticipation that she always felt when nearing the place.

Terry pressed her foot down harder on the accelerator, her shoulder-length hair flying about her face as she turned off the highway onto the blacktop road that would dead-end at the gates to the Triple L. In just a few more minutes she and the boys would finally be where they belonged, where she had always belonged. Feeling more carefree than she had in months, she drove past an endlessly shifting backdrop of steep summits, wild crags, narrow canyons, and tender meadows dotted by cattle.

"Whoo-pee-ti-yea," she burst out in song when she spotted the Triple L brand on a huge steer grazing near the barbed wire fence closest to the road. "Git along, little dogies."

At the unexpected sound of her voice, there was instant silence in the back seat, but then Chad declared knowingly, "We're almost there, Chuckie. Mom always sings that crazy song when we're coming to Grandpa Sam's."

The last time their mother had brought both boys out for a visit, Chuckie had just turned three and with one frightening exception, his memories of that vacation were somewhat vague. "I don't like doggies," he complained, his bottom lip quivering, and she knew he was remembering the litter of six black Labrador puppies who'd jumped up on him and licked him all over his face.

"Not doggies, you dummy. Mom said dogies," Chad hooted, a very superior expression on his round, freckled face as he punched his younger brother in the arm. "Dogies are cows. Every good cowboy knows that."

This announcement obviously didn't please Chuckie in the least, for he'd been to the petting zoo enough times to know that cows were much bigger than dogs. Sliding onto the floor of the car, he covered his reddish blond curls with his arms and started screaming, "If they lick me, I don't wanna be a cowboy. I don't wanna! I don't wanna!"

"You are one. You are one," Chad singsonged in rhythm with his brother's tearful cries. "We're living on a ranch so you are one. Ha...ha...ha."

"Enough!" Terry shrieked, outdoing both boys in volume. "Chuckie, you don't have to be anything you don't want to be, and Chad, if I ever again hear you calling your brother a dummy, you won't be able to sit down for a month."

Since neither of her sons had ever received a single spanking, she knew Chad wasn't frightened by that meaningless threat, but he still apologized to Chuckie and helped him fasten his seat belt once he'd climbed back up on the seat.

With a last, self-pitying sniff, Chuckie offered, "Mommy, I'll try to be brave if one licks me."

Chad was quick to declare, "Don't worry, Bro. If any old cow tries to lick you, I'll kick him."

"You will?" Chuckie inquired doubtfully.

"Right in the rump," Chad promised fiercely.

Brown eyes sparkling, Chuckie started singing. "Whoopteea, kick those dogies."

Chad immediately chimed in with another fractured lyric from a different song. "We'll bury a cow...on the lone prairie."

Terry didn't particularly approve of her eldest's solution to the cow licking problem, but she had to admire the results. As they passed through the ranch gates and rounded the curve that would bring the beloved, white clapboard house into view, both boys were wailing like a couple of banshees. Considering the fact that banshees were thought to be spirits who stood outside houses to warn someone inside of their impending doom, Terry was smiling slightly herself. She hoped Jesse Hubbard was listening and he'd better be listening good, for he was about to discover that some superstitions were based on fact.

Jess leaned back against the fireplace mantel in the living room, maintaining his distance as he watched the reunion taking place in the front hallway. He wanted to laugh when he saw the kind of punishment being meted out to Sam. The eldest boy had the old man's neck in a stranglehold and was clinging to him like a limpet, while the youngest one was crying and backing away, obviously terrified that Sam might try to touch him. The louder the kid cried, the more horrified Sam's expression became and the greater his efforts to reach him. Finally the little boy tripped over his own feet and fell down. Then the howling began in earnest.

As far as Jess was concerned, Sam deserved far worse than what he was getting, but the child's mother quickly leaned down and helped the boy back up to his feet. "It's all right, Precious," she crooned, patting the girlish, red-blond ringlets on the youngster's head while he wrapped his chubby arms around her waist and hid his tearful face in her pale green, pleated skirt. "Grandpa Sam didn't mean to frighten you, Chuckie. All he wanted was a hug. He hasn't seen you for such a long time, and he's really missed you."

"That I have," Sam assured, though his tone sounded almost as uncertain as the doubtful expression on "precious" little Chuckie's blotchy face. Of course, Jess concluded unsympathetically, since the older kid seemed determined to choke him, the hesitation in Sam's voice might have been caused by a lack of oxygen.

"Chuckie's very shy," the woman excused, dragging the reluctant boy with her as she walked over to Sam and bestowed a quick kiss on his weather-beaten cheek. "But we're all so very happy to finally be here. Aren't we, Chad?"

For the first time since the threesome had walked through the front door, the seven-year-old loosened his hold on his great grandfather's neck and allowed himself to be put back down. "We sure are," he agreed. "Can we go out and see the horses now?"

"Later, Chad," the woman said and turned to face the living room, giving Jess his first frontal view of her. "We have a few other things to do first."

As he watched her walk through the wide arch, Jess tried not to appear as stunned as he felt. He'd expected the elegant wardrobe, the smart designer traveling suit, those expensive white leather pumps and the twenty-four caret gold jewelry. He'd expected the salon haircut and tastefully understated makeup. What he hadn't expected was a woman who could take a man's breath away without the aid of any of those things.

Jess knew that his mouth was hanging open, but he couldn't prevent his astonished reaction to the sight of her. In his mind's eye, he'd pictured Terry Brubacker as a much younger and female version of Sam, but it was obvious that this woman hadn't inherited her looks from the Lawson side of the family. Unlike Sam, who was short and wiry, she was tall, at least five foot ten, and she didn't have Sam's nondescript facial features or grayish eye color. Terry's eyes were definitely

brown, a dark vivid brown, fringed by long sooty
lashes, but it wasn't those exotic looking eyes that
robbed Jess of breath. Nor was it her wide, sensual
mouth, aristocratic nose, and glossy black hair.

It was her spectacular body!

Sam's granddaughter wasn't just taller than most
females. She had a mind-boggling set of curves, a voluptuous figure that would heat any man's blood, and
Jess responded to her like any normal, red-blooded
man. As his eyes centered on the deep V in her blouse,
he felt a heavy throbbing in the lower regions of his
body. Beneath the splashy silk print, her breasts were
full and firm, a perfect fit for his large hands.

As soon as that thought occurred to him, Jess felt
his palms begin to sweat, but he needn't have worried
about it. The woman made no attempt to shake the
hand he offered her when Sam introduced them. She
acknowledged him and his outstretched hand only
briefly before they were both distracted by Chad's in-
sistence that he and his brother be allowed to visit the
barn.

"C'mon, Mom. We want to go outside."

"You told us we could see the horses," Chuckie reminded her with equal fervor.

"You promised, Mom." Chad quickly added his
validation of that claim. "You promised us and we
gotta go out there now cuz it's getting dark."

"If we don't go now, we'll go in the morning,"
Terry said, but the boys considered that offer totally
unacceptable.

Jess listened to their whining and Terry's placating
for a few more seconds before he lost his patience.

"Knock it off, fellas. You heard your mother. If you don't get to the barn tonight, you can see the horses in the morning."

Both boys promptly started bawling.

"I said stop it!" Jess bellowed, and his order was immediately followed by a blessed silence.

Unfortunately Jess didn't feel blessed for very long. Instead of thanking him, Terry Brubacker whirled back around, drew herself up to her full height, and declared, "Please don't raise your voice to them, Mr. Hubbard. They're just tired."

Jess opened his mouth to replace that assessment with one he considered far more apt, but then he saw the contempt in the woman's dark eyes, and his mouth snapped shut. Terry was looking at him as if he were some kind of criminal! Then he remembered that her opinion about him had little to do with reality, and everything to do with what a traitorous old man had led her to believe.

Sensing that Jess was about to blow a gasket, the traitor in question stepped forward with a hasty suggestion. "Would you mind bringing in the luggage, Jess?"

After a long pregnant pause, Jess nodded curtly and headed for the front door.

"Thank you, Mr. Hubbard," Terry called after him, and Jess clenched his teeth. The woman's frigidly polite tone conveyed something far different than her eternal gratitude, and it was obvious that she wanted him to know it.

"No problem," he returned coldly, letting her know that her message was received.

Two

Jess stretched out naked on the hard mattress, one hand resting under his head, the other on his chest, his fingers toying absently with the lucky gold piece he wore on a chain around his neck. He heard the downstairs grandfather clock chime midnight as he stared up at the narrow crack in the ceiling of his bedroom, then the tinkling bell that heralded the passing of another quarter hour. Okay, Hubbard, her opinion of you doesn't matter, he reminded himself, so you can relax.

Unfortunately the rigid muscles in his body stubbornly refused to comply with the well-intentioned advice of his brain. No matter what he tried telling himself, he was too damned angry to relax, and since Terry Brubacker and those whiny little brats of hers were now inhabiting the two spare bedrooms down the hall, it was safe to say that his disposition wasn't going to improve any by morning. Jess forced back the curse that threatened to burst forth from his mouth whenever he thought about his newest partner, fearing that the slightest sound would set those two mamma's boys of hers off on another round of caterwauling for which he, of course, would be blamed.

"Please don't raise your voice to them like that, Mr. Hubbard. They're just tired," he quoted the polite words under his breath, but his mind was focused on the condemning gaze that had accompanied that soft-spoken admonition. *Shut up, you bum!* That's what the woman had really wanted to say. *A lowlife like you has no right to even speak to my children.*

Over the years Jess had been called by any number of names, and even he had to admit that some of the more uncomplimentary descriptions had fit, but in all that time, no one had ever accused him of being dishonest. It was obvious that Terry believed he'd pulled off some kind of a swindle, but the deal he'd made with Sam was more than fair. With both the bank and the government on his tail, Sam had been close to losing the ranch. It would've been easy for Jess to take advantage of the situation, but he hadn't. Even back in the days when he hadn't had more than two nickels to rub together, though the opportunity had presented itself numerous times, he'd never once been tempted to use another man's misfortune to line his own pockets.

He was a Hubbard, dammit, and a Hubbard didn't lie, cheat, or steal!

Normally Jess didn't care what people assumed about him, right or wrong, but that was before he'd gazed wonderingly into a beautiful pair of brown eyes only to find out that their sexy owner considered him a shifty bushranger with no redeeming virtues at all. Terry Brubacker had condemned him to purgatory with those eyes, and for some reason, that silent condemnation bothered Jess more than if she'd come right out and called him a shyster to his face. At least then he'd have had the chance to dispute her unspoken accusations, fill her in on a few pertinent facts that her grandpa had deliberately neglected to tell her.

"For all the good that would've done me," Jess muttered, for it was just as apparent that the woman wouldn't have believed a single word he had to say. That knowledge twisted his insides and provoked a painful, burning sensation that he hadn't felt so strongly since Lottie Jean Hollister had thrown him over for a richer, more respectable man. He'd loved Lottie Jean with all of his heart and had assumed that she'd loved him in return, but he'd soon discovered that love didn't have the power to conquer all. When given the choice between happiness and money, Lottie had chosen money, having no faith in his ability to make something of himself.

Young fool that he'd been at the time, he'd begged her to reconsider, pleaded for a chance to prove himself, but nothing he'd said had convinced her that he'd be successful one day. Lottie Jean had left him with his pride in shreds, but she'd been the last female to accomplish that feat. Since then, he'd run across several other beautiful women who'd judged him on the size of his wallet or the kind of job he'd held down, but Lottie was the only one who could honestly claim that she'd completely humbled him.

He was older now, wiser, and a lot more cynical where women were concerned. He didn't have to be taught the same lesson twice. As long as he didn't expect anything from the female of the species but sexual satisfaction, he was rarely disappointed. Even those beauties who'd been ashamed to be seen with him during the day had eagerly sought out his bed at night, most anxious to make up to him for their hypocrisy. Since Jess hadn't particularly cared how they felt about him outside of the bedroom, he'd been content to let them try.

Why then, he was forced to ask himself, did Terry Brubacker's opinion bother him so much?

Unable to find an acceptable answer to that question, Jess rolled silently off the bed and pulled on a pair of jeans. Deciding that a healthy swig of whiskey would settle him down enough to sleep, he reached for the doorknob, then paused to make sure the soft click hadn't caused a stir. When his entrance into the dark hallway didn't incite a major riot in the back bedroom, he crept slowly toward the rickety stairs, resenting each and every carefully executed footstep. It was a damned sorry state of affairs when a grown man had to walk around on his tiptoes just to get somewhere in his own house!

Once he'd made it safely downstairs, Jess thought he and his bare feet were home free, but at the door to the kitchen, he ran smack-dab into trouble. "Ouch!" he cried out in agony when a pointed heel dug into his big toe, but that wasn't the worst of it. As a silk clad thigh slid between his legs and a pair of exquisitely soft, marvelously full breasts flattened against his chest, he was instantly aware of a throbbing pain in another part of his anatomy.

Upon impact, the feminine body struggled frantically to right itself, and in so doing, allowed Jess to feel a multitude of glorious sensations all at once. Not the least of which was her scent.

Terry Brubacker smelled just like she looked—disturbingly sensual, slightly mysterious, and delightfully spicy. Before his hands closed around the smooth skin of her bare arms, Jess took a deep breath and savored the captivating fragrance. Within seconds, he also learned that her tall, slender figure fit perfectly against his six and a half foot frame and every male instinct was telling him to do something about it.

Painfully aware of just how long he'd gone without a woman, he set Terry away from him with an abruptness that left her gasping. "Damnation, woman!" he swore. "What the hell are you doing down here anyway?"

"Well, excuse me, Mr. Hubbard," the indignant woman sputtered, as Jess reached behind him to flick on the light switch. "I've got just as much right to be in this kitchen as you do!"

"That's a matter of opinion," Jess growled, feeling as if he'd just taken a series of debilitating blows to his solar plexus. The least Sam could've done was warn him that his granddaughter packed such a sexy wallop. Maybe then his head wouldn't be reeling as if he were punch-drunk.

Refusing to let her see that the feel of her luscious body against his had knocked him totally off kilter, Jess hopped on one foot to the nearest chair. As he sat down to survey the damage to his injured toe, he caught sight of the feathery pink puffs peeking out from beneath the hem of Terry's matching night-gown, and all he could do was shake his head.

"What the devil do you think this is?" he inquired thickly, unable to stop his heated gaze from ascend-ing upward from her fancy slippers, admiring the fantastically long legs, womanly hips, and full breasts outlined in shimmering, hot pink silk. "A ranch house or a bordello?"

"What!"

"That getup sure doesn't leave much to the imagi-nation, not that I mind, of course," Jess drawled hatefully, finding that the fiery color in her cheeks had a very soothing effect on him. Taking a perverse en-joyment in that discovery, he continued, "You really can't blame me for wondering if you've forgotten where you are."

As soon as he said it, Jess found out that the woman did blame him for wondering any such thing. Just as she had when they met, Terry smote him with those smoky brown eyes of hers. "I know exactly where I am, Mr. Hubbard, and I also know exactly what kind of man I'm with . . . a low-down . . . conniving—"

Jess cut her off brutally before she could complete her faulty estimation of his character. "If that's how you feel, honey, you must really be desperate for a man. Or do you have the same reaction to every lowlife you happen to encounter?'' he said as his eyes dropped to her chest.

For a moment Terry just stood there staring, seemingly struck dumb. Jess could see her throat working, but even after several seconds, no words came out. Evidently too outraged to speak, she turned on one totally inappropriate heel and flounced out of the room.

Considering the fury in her parting glare, Jess doubted that she'd appreciate knowing how much he'd enjoyed his ringside view of her huffy exit. He was positive she didn't realize that high heels emphasized the provocative motion of a woman's backside when she walked, and Terry Brubacker had one of the sexiest wiggles he'd ever seen.

For the first time since setting eyes on the woman, Jess smiled with pleasure. So Ms. High and Mighty Brubacker could still blush, could she? At least there would be some compensations for her unwelcome presence in his house, and for the moment, those lovely compensations had soothed the savage beast far better than a swig of strong whiskey. As soon as he found a bandage for his aching toe, he was going to head straight back to bed for a good night's sleep.

Terry didn't care who she woke up as she stormed up the stairs to her bedroom and pulled out the only suitcase she hadn't had shipped by moving truck from under the bed. Even if the boys had woken up and come searching for her, they would've been far too frightened by her rage to confront her. The mother they knew never got so angry that she threw things, but clothing went flying as Terry searched for what she should've chosen to wear to bed in the first place, something that wouldn't titillate that gutter-minded turkey downstairs.

Jess Hubbard had made it sound as if sashaying around men in sexy nightclothes was her usual practice, but he was about to learn otherwise. It was obvious what kind of women he was used to associating with, but besides being a lady, she was the mother of two impressionable, young boys, and she wasn't about to tolerate some detestable, if great looking outlaw making sleazy insinuations about her moral character.

Great looking! Terry didn't know where that errant thought had come from, but the instant her subconscious mind brought it forth, her hands started shaking so badly that she had a hard time pulling on her sweatshirt and tightening the drawstring on her sweatpants.

"Okay," she acknowledged out loud, when her heartbeat simply refused to slow down. "The man's gorgeous, but that's not going to stop me from setting him straight on a few things."

Unfortunately her voice was no more steady than her hands, and she refused to confront her adversary in such a weakened condition. She had to regain control of herself, and the only way to do that, she told herself in her usual pragmatic manner, was to sit down on the bed and wait for the aftershocks of that outrageous encounter in the kitchen to pass. To her dismay, the more she thought about the incident, the more light-headed she felt.

Was it true what he'd said? Was she so desperate for a man, any man, that her slumbering libido could jump-start like that at the mere sight of a bare chest? Had two years' worth of sexual deprivation robbed her of all moral discretion?

"Absolutely not," she declared emphatically, taking pity on herself. She was a normal woman with a normal sexual appetite, and under the same set of circumstances, any woman would've suffered a violent physical reaction. After all, she concluded self-righteously, we aren't talking about just any chest here. We're talking perfect chest...and a flat stomach...and lean hips...and taut, muscular thighs.

"Damn and blast!" Terry whispered, furious with herself for being unable to stop remembering how she'd felt pressed up so intimately against that big, gloriously made, male body. She'd long since broken contact with it, but her breasts still felt swollen and tender. Even now her fingertips tingled with tactile memory of those smooth, well-defined pectorals, that soft crinkly chest hair, and her legs still quivered in reaction to the feel of those rock-hard thighs encased in faded denim.

Of course, she hadn't meant to arouse the urgent male power she'd felt pressed against her when they were in close contact, but her treacherous body hadn't seemed to care that its enjoyment came about by accident. Her nipples had tightened sharply beneath the silk bodice of her gown, and she'd felt a throbbing pleasure deep inside her womb, a momentary spasm of such unexpected force that when he'd thrust her away from him, she'd just stood there, gasping for breath.

She might have managed to maintain her dignity if Jess hadn't decided that they needed more light on the situation. As soon as he'd flicked on the wall switch, she'd discovered the insolent way he was gazing at her, and her body betrayed her once more. It was as if she'd suddenly been struck dumb, unable to do anything but stare mutely back at him as he'd leisurely admired every curve she had to offer.

Before that moment she hadn't looked at him closely enough to see that his shoulders were amazingly broad, that his hair shone like newly minted gold, or that his eyes were so deep a blue that it almost hurt her to look at them. Nor had she realized that his face was so tanned, and his features so ruthlessly handsome.

And that voice of his! All she had to do was think about that low, sexy rasp and her entire body was enveloped in heat. He'd spoken so slowly, each lazily drawled word searing into her like a brand, his husky tone reverberating along nerve endings that had already been oversensitized by their scintillating contact with his warm, bare skin. Up until that nerve-shattering moment, she'd never viewed Jess Hubbard as a flesh and blood man, only as the sneaky skulker who'd taken advantage of her grandfather when he was down.

"And that's exactly who he is," Terry reminded herself in a desperate whisper, the anger she'd been harboring ever since Sam had called to inform her that he'd sold out half the Triple L to some stranger, swiftly coming back to the fore.

Seconds later she had fully recovered from her shameful attack of lust and was prepared to fight. Armored in navy blue jersey that was baggy enough to camouflage all signs of her gender, she marched back down the stairs. With her head held high and her dark eyes fired by the light of battle, she advanced across enemy lines into the kitchen.

"Now *I'm* going to tell *you* something, buster," she said, stalking to where Jess was still seated on the same chair, one foot propped up as he bandaged his toe. "Make those suggestive kind of remarks to me again and I won't just step on your foot, I'll cut you off at the knees!"

At first, Terry was too caught up in her own zeal to notice that her tirade wasn't having the desired effect on her adversary, but then she saw his upper lip twitch, and she lost it completely. Unmindful of the possible consequences to such an action, she lifted her hand, using one finger to poke him in the chest as she berated, "I'm warning you, right now, Jess Hubbard. I won't tolerate that kind of smutty talk around my children. Do you hear me?"

The woman was making a habit of catching him off guard, but Jess was becoming very familiar with his reaction. Her sultry dark looks, biting words, and unjust deeds irritated the hell out of him and incited a violent impulse that he'd worked long and hard to overcome. Sometimes, however, given enough abuse, even a peace-loving man crossed over the line, and for Jess, this was one of those times.

With the speed of a striking rattler, he reached out and grabbed her wrist, stopping her finger in mid-poke. "And I'm warning you, do that again and those tender ears upstairs are going to hear every foul word in the English language!"

For several long moments after that announcement neither of them said a word, but then Jess realized that his grip on her wrist was too tight. Horrified that he'd hurt her, he thrust her arm away from him, his coloring as pale as hers as he stood up from the chair.

Terry jerked away from him so quickly that she almost lost her balance and had to grip the edge of the table to keep herself from falling. Immediately contrite, Jess was about to apologize, but when he met her disdainful gaze, the words refused to come. In the heat of the moment he'd forgotten that in her eyes, he'd already been tried, convicted, and hung out to dry.

Furious with her for prejudging him so unfairly, he growled, "Like it or not, lady, I stepped in and saved Sam's hide."

"Saved *his* hide?" Terry pooh-poohed that ridiculous notion. "From what I hear, the only hide you care about is your own."

Jess was primed for a fight as much she was, but when she looked down her aristocratic nose at him, he immediately lost the urge to defend himself. If her accusation hadn't convinced him, her hoity-toity attitude proved that she considered herself his social and intellectual superior. That being so, the few choice words he had in mind to say would only verify her opinion. On the other hand, if she expected him to tuck his tail between his legs and slink away like some mangy mongrel, she could just think again.

"Since you're shooting in the dark, I'm willing to forget we had this little skirmish," he stated coldly. "But lady, if you ever take me on like this again, you're going to regret it."

"I regret the necessity of even speaking to the likes of you," Terry retorted scathingly, refusing to cower beneath his macho threat. "But to get your filthy hands off this property, I'm willing to do almost anything."

His gaze passed over her figure, lingering suggestively on the curves even a baggy sweatshirt couldn't hide. "Anything?" he inquired silkily.

Terry was so angry, she felt as if her insides were burning up, yet at the same time, she felt more alive than she had in a year. During the long, drawn out process of her divorce she'd awed her lawyer and amazed her closest friends by always maintaining her cool, even when the sordid, humiliating details of her husband's extramarital affair had been aired in court for all to hear. By the time Doug had demonstrated his total lack of respect for her by offering a settlement that was less than what she'd receive by going on welfare, the wall of ice around her heart had become so thick that she'd managed to turn him down without the slightest show of heat.

For months now she'd suppressed her rage, hidden the devastating hurt and nearly intolerable pain behind that icy wall, but the hot gaze of an uncivilized, insolent cowboy had blasted through every frozen layer, unleashing emotions so violent that her voice shook. "You really are immoral, aren't you?"

Jess didn't respond to that charge by so much as a blink, but before giving her his back, Terry saw a flash of something besides anger in his eyes. Unbelievably, that something looked very much like hurt, which prompted her to ask if it were possible to hurt the feelings of a heartless scoundrel? Terry didn't think so, yet she was almost positive that the man had been sincerely wounded by her insults.

As for Jess, he didn't care if they ever shared another conversation, but he did want the last word in this one. "Believe me, I regret the deal came down this way every bit as much as you do."

Oddly enough, Terry did believe him, and that not only deflated her anger, but forced her to question someone else's character. Until her grandfather had dropped the bombshell that he'd sold half of the ranch at a questionable price to some drifter who'd arrived out of nowhere, she hadn't yet made up her mind about moving herself and the children back to Montana. Was it possible that Grandpa Sam had deliberately misled her in order to force the issue? She opened her mouth, intending to pursue that possibility, but Jess had already left the room.

The longer Terry stared at the empty doorway the more imperative her need became to speak to Grandpa Sam. Terry knew it was very late, almost 1 a.m. in the morning, but she wouldn't be able to sleep a wink unless these nagging doubts of hers were put firmly to rest.

With that goal in mind, she walked down the back

hall off the kitchen. "Wake up, Grandpa," she called knocking on the door to the only first floor bedroom. "It's Terry, and we need to talk."

Three

The moving truck arrived on the following Monday, confirming the fact that Brubacker and Sons were now permanent residents of the Triple L. To be honest, Jess had to admit that most of Terry's furniture, especially that soft, buff-colored leather living room set, was more stylish and in much better shape than anything he and Sam owned. Still, Jess didn't much appreciate the visual proof of Terry's presence that could be found in almost every room of the house, and he went out of his way to avoid using her furnishings.

Actually, for the past week, he'd avoided the house altogether. Before the unwelcome trio had arrived, his plans to reconstruct the ranch's outdated network of fences, corrals, and chutes into a more efficient pattern had pretty much remained on the drawing board. Since then, however, he'd spent every spare minute of his time actually working on the project, starting with the erection of a branding corral to replace the broken-down one in the north pasture. Back in the good old days, he and Sam would've discussed what chores they intended to tackle during the day over a hot break-fast, but now, Jess made it a practice to roll out of bed long before sunup, wolf down a couple of baloney sandwiches, and ride out to the range before anyone else was awake.

Thus far, this modus operandi had succeeded on two levels. He was close to completing construction on the new holding pen, and in the week since Terry's ar-rival, he'd successfully managed to avoid all but the briefest of contacts with her. Considering the fact that they shared the same house, Jess realized that even-tually he'd be forced to deal with the maddening woman again, but reflecting upon their last confron-tation, which he did with annoying regularity, he was content to postpone that occasion for as long as pos-sible.

Unfortunately Jess had to admit that there was also a downside to this self-enforced isolation policy, the most negative aspect being his lack of three square meals a day. Skipping the noonday meal made it pos-sible for him to avoid the homefront until sunset, but the practice had already cost him a few more pounds than he could afford, and the louder his stomach growled, the more irritable he became. Whether or not he was actually hungry, he felt like chewing nails most of the time.

Today, instead of using his hammer to alleviate his frustration and work past the gnawing ache in his belly, he found himself leaning back against a fence post and daydreaming about the leftover beef stew that he'd discovered in the refrigerator that morning. Sam might have been right in saying that his granddaughter was a good cook, especially if that stew tasted as delicious as it had looked and smelled. If, for a change, Terry and her kids went to bed at a normal hour instead of staying up late to watch some stupid movie on their VCR, he might even get to taste that savory concoction before he passed out from starvation.

Praying for a miracle, Jess took a nail out of his mouth and, with two strokes of his hammer, pounded it into the top rail of the corral. After strong-arming a second nail, then a third, he lifted a gloved hand and tilted the sweat-stained brim of his black Stetson so he could squint up at the brilliant blue spring sky. According to the position of the sun, it was less than an hour past noon, yet his stomach already felt as if it were feeding on itself.

With renewed force, Jess abused some more nails, smashing their heads into the rail as he pictured Sam sitting down at the kitchen table about to enjoy a hearty, home-cooked meal. The image was so clear in his mind that by the time he'd finished pulling out all the nails he'd pounded in at the wrong angle, he was feeling infinitely more sorry for himself. If that old man had been any kind of a friend to him at all, he would've packed a lunch pail with whatever food he hadn't downed himself and brought it out to the pasture for Jess to eat. Sam knew damned well what it was like to work all day on an empty stomach. After enduring a week of such torture, Jess was beginning to think that his fair-weather partner didn't have an ounce of compassion in his scrawny body.

"Don't you think this has gone on long enough?"

"Ouch!" Jess peeled off his calfskin glove and whirled around, cussing unintelligibly as he sucked on the throbbing pulp that had recently been his left thumb. Through a red haze of pain, he watched Terry Brubacker climb down from Sam's big bay gelding and walk toward him, and even though his vision was blurred, he could see that she looked just as good in blue jeans as she had in pink silk. Maybe better, for the designer jeans were so tight that her statuesque figure was outlined far more accurately than it had been that night in the kitchen. When Jess added those newfound statistics to the voluptuous curves delightfully emphasized by her tailored white blouse, he didn't just feel hot under the collar but below the belt as well.

In no mood to suffer in silence, he held up his injured digit and swore, "Damnation, woman! Look what you made me do!"

"I'm so sorry," Terry apologized, but the odd set to her mouth made Jess think that she was less than sincere, was in fact, doing her best not to laugh.

That possibility incensed him and inspired his next outburst. "What the hell are you doing here anyway?"

And then she did. She threw back her glorious head of silky black hair and laughed uproariously. Since no woman on earth had ever dared laugh in the face of his anger, Jess didn't quite know how to react, so he just stood there, glaring impotently, until she shut up long enough to notice that he wasn't joining in with her amusement.

"Either you've got an extremely limited vocabulary, Mr. Hubbard, or a short memory," Terry teased good-naturedly, determined to get on his best side. "As I recall, the last time we met you asked me that very same question in that exact same tone of voice."

Jess didn't care for her reminder of that disastrous event anymore than he appreciated her intimation that he might not be of sound mind. His extreme displeasure was evident as he growled. "Since I now have a sore thumb to go along with my sore toe, I'd say the same speech still applies. As far as I'm concerned, Mrs. Brubacker, you're a health hazard."

Terry's expression was both injured and insulted. "It's not my fault that you keep hurting yourself!"

"If you didn't make a habit of showing up in places where you don't belong, neither one of us would have to get hurt."

It was patently obvious to Terry that the man wasn't talking about her arrival in the pasture today, but of her presence in general, and that ignited her temper. "I belong on this ranch, Mr. Hubbard, every bit as much, if not more than you do!"

"Like hell."

Terry's shoulders drooped slightly as she reconsidered the thoroughly disagreeable task she'd set forth for herself today. Apologizing to this big surly brute was not only going to be one of the hardest things she'd ever done, it just might turn out to be impossible. The man wasn't only insufferably rude. He also had no sense of humor. Obviously she wasn't the only one who had a major problem with the uncomfortable situation Grandpa Sam had created for them, but at least she was willing to behave pleasantly until the problem was resolved.

"I'm sorry you feel that way, and I'm truly sorry that you hurt yourself," she conceded, hoping she wouldn't choke on the lie.

Jess grunted in response to her words, then he made a dramatic show of bandaging himself, audibly wincing and gritting his teeth as he wrapped his kerchief around his thumb.

Terry did not make a very sympathetic audience. According to Casey Turner, a childhood friend who she had run into on a recent trip into town, Jess Hubbard was reputed to be a hard-bitten, macho cowboy. Surely that type of man was supposed to be impervious to the everyday aches and pains in life, but in Terry's opinion, when it came to even the most minor of injuries, Mister Macho here acted like a great big baby. Still, if she were going to accomplish what she'd set out to do, she really had no choice but to appease him.

"Believe me, Jess," she insisted, striving for a remorseful tone. "I never meant for this to happen, and I do hope you don't suffer any lasting impairment."

Terry's overly contrite apology made it sound to Jess as if she were blaming herself for causing him some permanent disability, and that ridiculous notion wounded his ego. Unlike this tall, slender woman with the delicate wrists, he didn't possess a fragile bone in his body. It should've been obvious to her that she couldn't hurt him even if she tried. "Don't worry about it," he felt obliged to say. "I heal quick."

Terry pounced on that meager concession like a starving dog on a T-bone. "So you accept my apology?"

When Jess saw the eager expression on her face and the anxious look in her big brown eyes, his throat constricted and he had to swallow twice before he could talk. The woman might be a menace, but Lord, what she could do to him with those eyes. "Sure."

His positive tone gave Terry some hope that she wasn't pursuing a totally lost cause. When he even went so far as to return her tentative smile, she took another step closer to him and inquired, "Then can I also take it that you'd be willing to start this affair all over again?"

Affair! For the past several days Jess had been acutely aware that where this woman was concerned, his body was both willing and able to start an affair. Luckily his befuddled brain still had enough sense left to conclude that her inquiry had nothing to do with a sudden desire on her part to rip off all her clothes and jump his bones.

"What affair?" he managed to ask, hoping she didn't recognize the raspy note in his voice for what it actually was.

"You know...." Terry shrugged her slender shoulders, then with an awkward motion, thrust out her hand appealingly. "Truce?"

Highly suspicious of her sudden change in attitude, Jess retreated a step, but Terry misinterpreted his action, especially when he thrust his injured hand behind his back. Feeling guilty for labeling him as a crybaby, she reached behind him and retrieved his clenched fist. "Oh dear, does it really hurt that much?"

The instant she touched him, Jess felt a strong jolt of sensation that had nothing to do with the throbbing pain in his thumb. Electricity shot up his arm and vibrated across his chest. A second later the shock reached his middle. He felt his stomach drop down to his toes and then a hot, pooling sensation fill the vacated space.

His entire body broke out in a sweat. It was crazy...irrational. He couldn't stand this woman, but he wanted her...badly. Right here and right now!

Blankly, Jess stared at the soft, feminine hand clasping his own, stunned by the knowledge that the mere touch of her long elegant fingers could set off such a gut-wrenching response deep down inside him. More to himself than to her, he insisted. "I'm just fine."

"Let me see," Terry said, unaware that Jess considered himself a defenseless victim faced with a woman who was armed and highly dangerous. As he struggled to muster his wildly scattered defenses, she disarmed him even further by gently uncurling the fist that hid his hurt thumb from her view. "It's certainly swollen. Maybe you've fractured the bone."

Overwhelmed by her tender treatment, Jess wanted to snatch his hand out of her grasp, but he couldn't even muster the strength to protest when she led him meekly away from the pasture fence and back in the direction of her horse. Once there, she suggested,

"Why don't you sit down on this grassy patch and make yourself comfortable?"

Letting go of his hand, she reached for a saddle-bag. "I'll check to see if Sam's gear contains anything useful besides your lunch, like a first aid kit. If not, maybe we can find a stick around here to use as a splint."

Before regaining any degree of his normal comprehension, Jess found himself seated cross-legged in the grass. When he was finally able to think properly again, he exclaimed, "You brought me my lunch!"

Terry shook her head and her expression was chagrined as she lifted the saddlebag off the horse and untied the blanket she'd brought along to spread out on the ground for their picnic. "It's the least I could do. Considering how little you ate for breakfast this morning, you must be very hungry by now."

"Mmm," Jess mumbled his agreement, but his eyes narrowed suspiciously. No matter how friendly she sounded, he still found this sudden outburst of good-will highly suspect. He'd been hungry yesterday, too, and the day before that, but Terry hadn't brought out something for him to eat then. Obviously the woman was after something, but what?

"I should have done this several days ago," Terry admitted, as if she'd just read his mind and understood his doubts about her. "But I've had a very difficult time working up the courage to face you again."

Jess scowled at that comment, remembering how quickly she'd jumped away from him that night after he'd accidentally hurt her wrist. Knowing she disliked him was one thing, he could deal with that possibility, but he didn't like knowing that she saw him as some kind of brutal ogre. Hurting women, even one who heartily deserved it, wasn't his way. "You're afraid of me?"

Terry peered over her shoulder at him, one dark, feathery brow lifted in utter disdain. "Don't be silly."

The woman was lying and Jess refused to let her get away with it. "I know fear when I see it, and you were afraid of me that night."

"Afraid of what I might do if you didn't back off. Under the circumstances, you're lucky I didn't give you a black eye," Terry retorted, unable to back down from his provoking challenge. Never in her life had she met a more infuriating man, nor one who could antagonize her without even half trying. And that was a realization that made it even more difficult to remain in control. After all she'd been through with Doug, she hated the thought that any man could rile her this way, but Jess Hubbard had a real talent for making her see red.

Jess saw the flashing sparks of temper in her eyes, and a different kind of fire ignited deep inside him. "You're lucky I didn't give you . . ."

He didn't complete the threat, fearing that he was about to instigate a repeat of their last heated skirmish, but the unspoken knowledge of what he'd like to do with her swirled back and forth between them until Terry blushed like a nervous virgin and abruptly turned away. Noting her high color, Jess couldn't hold back the gratified smile that tugged at the corners of his mouth, or the speculative gleam that came into his eye when he pondered her reaction. Was Terry just as sexually aware of him as he was of her?

Terry didn't dare look at Jess again until she had the blanket spread out on the ground and had knelt down upon it. The hungry way he'd been looking at her had her heart pounding like a jackhammer, but if the fates were kind, once she'd provided him with two thick roast beef sandwiches, a plastic container of soup, three hard-boiled eggs, two apples, a half-dozen homemade chocolate chip cookies, and a large thermos of coffee, he'd start concentrating on the food instead of her.

At this point in her life, she wasn't ready to deal with a man's sexual hunger, even though she might suffer from a similar craving. It had taken her eight years to rectify the mistakes she'd made by marrying Doug, and she'd learned a few very painful lessons along the way. First and foremost, she knew that the next time she entered into a relationship with a man, if there ever was a next time, she'd be leading with her head, not her heart, and definitely not with her libido.

At eighteen, a girl could fool herself into believing that passion inevitably led to love, but at twenty-six, Terry knew better. "I hope this will be enough food to tide you over until suppertime."

Before she'd completed the sentence, Jess was already grabbing a sandwich. "This is great."

Terry's eyes widened as she watched him wolf down several bites. "From the grip you've got on that sandwich, I'd say your thumb isn't broken."

"I never said it was," Jess agreed between bites.

Terry rolled her eyes. "So you just wanted to make me feel guilty."

Jess's blue eyes twinkled. "Maybe," he acknowledged with a devilish grin that reminded Terry so much of Chad at his most mischievous that she found herself grinning back.

Several more seconds passed before she remembered that her reason for coming out here today was no cause for amusement. Forcing her thoughts back on track, she delayed making further conversation until Jess's mouth was too full to politely talk back, then she launched into the discussion she'd been practicing for several days.

"You haven't made this very easy on me, you know," she accused without force, admiring the ease in which he'd managed to avoid her all week. "I was all set to apologize for my misconceptions about you the very next morning, but you were already gone from the house and you've pretty much stayed gone ever since."

"Grpmph," Jess acknowledged.

Terry put her own interpretation on that unintelligible comment. "You were deliberately avoiding me," she agreed, sighing as she continued. "And after what Grandpa Sam told me, I really can't blame you. I do realize now that you're not exactly the total bad guy I was led to believe."

"Gee thanks," Jess muttered dryly, before making the strategic error of starting on his second sandwich.

"Come on, Jess, you have to admit that there are some very gaping holes in your personal history that would make any normal person wonder." Terry pointed out in defense of her admittedly faint praise. "No matter what Grandpa Sam thinks about you, and *he* thinks you can practically walk on water, I still believe he was very foolish for putting his complete trust in a total stranger like that. For all he knew at the time, you could've been a thief, or a con man, or something even worse."

"Grmph!"

"Still, I realize that if you hadn't made good on that bank note and paid off his back taxes when you did, Grandpa could've lost the ranch, and as you probably know by now, that might very well have killed him. I suppose I should be grateful to you for that, though I can't help thinking that if my divorce settlement had just come through a few months earlier, the Triple L would still be wholly owned by our family, and now we wouldn't be in this horrible fix."

Glancing up into a pair of blistering blue eyes, Terry added hastily, "Not that I think you're a horrible person, Jess. You just happened to be in the right place at the right time to make a fantastic deal. All I meant was that it would've been better for all concerned if I had been the one to rescue Grandpa Sam. Since I wasn't given the chance, we're now faced with a whole set of sticky complications."

Jess swallowed his last bite of sandwich without even chewing it. "Such as?"

Oblivious to the less than amiable tone of Jess's response, Terry charged ahead. She'd been pondering their situation for several days now and was certain that she'd found a solution that would be equitable to everyone. "As I see it, since we both know this partnership is never going to work out, the first problem we have to solve is how to finance its dissolution. I admit that it took me awhile to determine what was best for myself and the boys, but now that I've reached a decision concerning our future, I'm prepared to do whatever it takes to regain sole ownership of the ranch. The Triple L has been owned by the Lawson family for six generations, and that's a tradition I intend to uphold. Of course, I realize that you'll expect to make a decent profit from your short-term investment."

"Of course," Jess agreed, and even managed to gesture with his hand for Terry to proceed with her autocratic little speech. As soon as she'd showed up today, spouting apologies and bearing gifts, he'd known she was up to something, and now, if he could just keep a lid on his temper, he was going to find out exactly what it was. Indeed, the silly woman seemed eager to lay every one of her cards on the table as if she were betting on a sure thing, totally disregarding the fact that he was holding all the aces.

Jess stretched his legs out full length before him and reached for an apple before he leaned back on the blanket, resting the weight of his torso on one elbow. Terry assumed by his relaxed posture that he was prepared to listen, and she was relieved beyond measure. "You're going to be reasonable about this."

Jess grinned at the obvious surprise in her tone. "I'm not an unreasonable man."

Before offering any further details of her plan, Terry took out the extra mug she'd packed in the saddlebag and poured herself a cup of coffee. She no longer felt so nervous that she had to rattle off her entire spiel before he had a chance to interrupt, but her mouth still felt uncomfortably dry. She took a sip of coffee, then another restorative swallow.

Jess knew she was unaware of his fascinated gaze as her small pink tongue came out to lick a droplet of moisture from the corner of her delectable mouth. Nor did she notice the subtle change in his breathing pattern when she curled one long, shapely leg underneath her and leaned slightly forward for balance, a movement that shifted her blouse and allowed him an enticing glimpse of her French demicup bra.

"I've tried to look at this problem from all possible angles, and I believe I've come up with a way out of this situation that will benefit us both," Terry said, then just in case Jess was as chauvinistic as Grandpa Sam and had doubts about a woman's problem-solving ability, she promised, "After hearing me out I think you'll agree that I have a much better head for business than my grandfather."

As Terry continued talking in that low, sultry voice of hers, Jess was reminded of a line from the second run feature he'd watched at the Rialto on one of his rare trips into town. The blond, bosomy actress had leaned forward on her bar stool and murmured seductively to the handsome male actor admiring her cleavage, "I've got a head for business and a bod for sin. Do you have a problem with that?"

Unlike the actor, who'd portrayed a high-powered corporate trader, a good ol' country boy like himself had a mighty big problem handling a woman like that, and Terry Brubacker was definitely that kind of woman. As he watched the provocative movement of her lips, imagined what kissing her would feel like, several moments went by without him hearing a single thing she said. Not that it mattered, of course, for however 'beneficial' her offer, Jess had no intention of selling off his half of the Triple L.

"So what do you think?"

When Terry got no response to her question, she waited what she considered a reasonable length of time for Jess to make a decision, then rephrased it. "Do you find my proposition fair?"

"Fair?" Jess repeated blankly, then realized that Terry was finished talking to him. With a great deal of effort, he pushed away the sexual fantasy that had occupied his mind for the past several minutes, even though dealing with the real woman seated before him seemed a far less pleasant prospect than dealing with her gloriously naked, if imaginary counterpart.

"More than fair," he allowed, though he couldn't recall any specific terms. "If I had any intention of selling, which I don't."

Terry blinked, disbelieving her own ears. "You won't even consider it?"

"There's nothing to consider," Jess informed her bluntly, reverting to the hateful man Terry had thought he was before Grandpa Sam had convinced her otherwise. "I bought this place because it offered me the kind of challenge I've spent a long time searching for. The odds might be against me, but I'm going to make something of this place before I'm through. I've got big plans for it, and whatever you say, I'm not going to change them."

"You only bought fifty percent of the place. I own the other fifty," Terry snapped. "So how does that affect all your big plans?"

Jeff ignored her waspish question in order to pose a couple of his own, and considering how much she'd just revealed about herself, his tone was far more caustic than Terry's had been. "A little quick to put your grandpa in the grave, aren't you, honey? The way it was explained to me, you only own twenty-five percent. Does Sam know his loving granddaughter has him dead and buried already, or have you got that gullible old man tricked into believing that you don't see a bunch of dollar signs whenever you look at him?"

Horrified by the interpretation he'd placed on her unthinking comment, Terry jumped up from the blanket. "How dare you even suggest such a rotten thing! I love Grandpa Sam with all my heart! Why, he raised me from the time I was two and I owe the world to him!"

"Which is why you haven't even bothered to visit him until you heard he'd sold a share of this place to me. That's all you really care about, isn't it, Terry? Getting your share?"

"Why you . . . you . . ." Terry couldn't think of anything despicable enough to call him. Once again, he'd managed to make her speechless with rage. She tossed a half cup of cold coffee into his face, then threw down the empty mug and ran for her horse.

Jess didn't wipe the moisture from his face or even bother to stand up as Terry lifted one leg over the saddle and fit her heels into the stirrups. He leaned back on both elbows, feeling well-fed and well-satisfied. His day might have gotten off to a bad start, but things had definitely improved since then.

"Majority partner, boss, ramrod. I'll answer to any of those titles," he suggested smugly, and took another bite of his apple.

Terry guided the gelding closer to the blanket and jerked on the reins, prompting the horse to rear up on its hind legs. Then, in a show of horsemanship worthy of a top notch rodeo rider, she brought those pawing hooves back down within six inches of Jess's outstretched legs.

"When I'm through with you, Mister, you're going to answer for plenty!" she exclaimed, before she galloped off, leaving Jess to wonder if his airless lungs would ever again draw a normal breath.

Four

———

Ms. Terry Brubacker was an extremely sore loser, Jess grumbled to himself as he slipped stealthily into the horse barn and walked down the center aisle to the last stall on the left. For a second or two he assumed he was safe, but as soon as he picked up a curry brush, the barn door slid open behind him, and he sighed, resigned to the inevitable. Seeking revenge for his refusal to sell out to her, Terry had sicced her boys on him, and for the past two days, they'd dogged Jess's heels like a pair of pesky puppies. Every time he turned around, he found one or the other of them underfoot, hitting him with a barrage of questions, seemingly fascinated with every move he made.

Obviously this morning was to be no exception. He'd done his best to sneak out of the house without alerting his faithful watchdogs, but just like yesterday and the day before that, they'd nosed him out in a matter of minutes. Jess was beginning to think there was no escape for him anywhere.

"Whatcha doin', Jess?" Chad wanted to know as he stepped up on the bottom slat of the horse stall and hooked both of his arms over the top. As usual, his small freckled face was alight with curiosity, and his big brown eyes, the exact same shade as his mother's, sparkled eagerly.

"Brushing down my horse," Jess growled, his tone as cold and unwelcoming as he could make it. For all the good that did him, for in the next instant another voice was heard, a strident, demanding voice that startled Jess's big palomino stallion so much that the high-strung animal reared his head and almost knocked Jess off his feet.

"I wanna see! I wanna see!"

"Whoa, Dusty," Jess murmured soothingly, grasping the top edge of the stall with both hands as he struggled to keep his boots from sliding out from under him. "Settle down, boy. Settle down."

"I wanna see! I wanna see!"

Dusty sidestepped onto his foot and Jess roared, "Dammit, kid, pipe down! Jeezus, Mary, and Martha!"

To Jess's undying gratitude, both the shying horse and howling boy responded the same way to his vituperation. Standing stock-still, they expressed their hurt feelings with a series of indignant snorts and sniffles. Gritting his teeth, Jess limped out of the stall, still cursing under his breath as he reclosed the gate.

From his less than lofty perch on the horse stall, Chad scowled down at his five-year-old brother, matching Jess's ferocious expression. "Jeezus, Mary, and Martha, Chuckie," he mimicked enthusiastically. "I've had it with all this damned caterwauling."

As he listened to that discomfiting rendition of his own off-color vocabulary coming out of the mouth of a seven-year-old boy, Jess cast an uneasy glance over his shoulder, breathing a sigh of relief when he saw that a certain someone hadn't entered the barn unannounced. During his last hair-raising confrontation with Terry, he'd come close to losing the use of his legs, and he could only guess how violently she'd react to this touching little scene. Considering how protective she was of her precious darlings, he assumed that he'd probably be lucky to get off with his life.

Preventing that from happening would require some quick backtracking, Jess concluded grudgingly. "Come over here, Chuck," he requested, forcing himself to smile as he held out his hand to the tearful youngster. "I'll lift you up so you can see Dusty."

The child was clearly suffering from some highly conflicting emotions, but after staring down at his shiny new cowboy boots for several moments, curiosity finally won out over his fear. Though his lower lip was still quivering, he lifted his chin bravely, then lost most of his courage and mumbled into his chest. "Okay."

"Sorry I yelled at you, boy," Jess apologized, feeling like a complete louse when he saw a fat teardrop splash onto the cement floor of the barn. "I'm just not used to having little kids around."

"I didn't mean to scare your horse," Chuckie murmured haltingly, his big brown eyes opening very wide when Jess leaned down and scooped him up using only one arm. "Dusty's so way bigger than me, I thought nuthin' could scare him."

"Bigger doesn't always mean braver," Jess said, experiencing a very funny feeling in his chest as he felt two small arms creep up around his neck and a lock of baby-fine hair caress his stubbled cheek. "And it doesn't always mean older, either. Now, let's take poor Dusty here for example. He may be way bigger than you, but he's only four years old and a lot of things still scare him."

"Jeezus, Mary, and Martha," Chad exclaimed in astonishment. "Dusty's younger than Chuckie!"

"Uh . . . Chad, I think you'd better stop using that particular expression," Jess advised, shooting another nervous glance over his shoulder. "And you also have to quit saying dammit. If your mom ever hears you talking like that, she'll pitch a fit."

"But that's how you always talk," Chad replied with a child's irrefutable logic. "And when I grow up, I want to be a cowboy just like you."

Jess was about to squash that ridiculous notion in no uncertain terms, but when he saw the worshipful expression on Chad's face, he didn't have the heart to do it. Since he'd barely ever said a civil word to the boy, he couldn't understand why Chad was looking at him as if he were some kind of a superhero. Indeed, whenever the chattering twosome came around to bother him, he'd gone out of his way to act like a cantankerous old mustang with a burr under his saddle.

As he struggled to take in the boy's mind-boggling claim that he wanted to grow up to be just like him, Jess began to feel extremely ashamed of himself, and all he could think of to say was a husky, "You do, huh?"

"Me too, dammit," Chuck declared happily, and when the youngster accompanied that sunny announcement with a swift hug, a huge lump developed in Jess's throat. Okay, he admitted, maybe these boys could be pains in the neck on occasion, but they could also be very endearing.

"Will you teach us to be cowboys, Jess?" Chad inquired plaintively. "Will ya?"

"Will ya? Will ya?" Chuckie echoed.

Jess cleared his throat, reluctant to promote himself as any kind of role model. He was a loner, responsible to no one but himself, and that's the way he liked it. He understood that young boys needed to look up to somebody, but if he had anything to say about it, that person was not going to be him. "Wouldn't you guys rather grow up to be lawyers like your dad? It's a much better job, very exciting, and it pays a whole lot more money."

"I don't want to be any dumb old lawyer!" Chad declared emphatically, giving Jess a wounded look before he jumped down from his perch.

Securing Chuck against his shoulder, Jess stepped around the corner of Dusty's stall, but not in time to catch Chad who was already running back down the center aisle. Grim-faced, Jess strode after him. For the past two days, he'd tried everything imaginable to get rid of his constant shadows, unaware that the mere mention of the boys' father would do the job, and now that he'd stumbled upon the right tactic, he wished he could rip out his thoughtless tongue.

Sam had told him that Terry's divorce had been bitter, and he should have realized that her sons had witnessed at least some of the turmoil that had taken place between their parents. If that were true, then it would also follow that they would be tempted to choose sides. Jess had erroneously assumed that the boys were too young to make damning judgments against either one of their parents, but Chad had just proved him wrong on that score. As he watched the boy's frantic but ineffectual efforts to push open the heavy barn door, Jess figured that psychology might be a wiser means of persuasion than physical force.

Stopping in front of the horse stall closest to the door, he pointed to a black and white dappled mare and informed Chuck, "If you really want to be a cowboy, kid, you'll have to learn how to ride a horse, and Brandy's the best one we've got for teaching beginners. She's very gentle and has a lot of patience."

Then he added the statement that was certain to prick the interest of another little boy. "If your mom says it's okay, I'll give you your first lesson this morning."

Chuck didn't look entirely too sure that he wanted a riding lesson, but Chad immediately stopped pushing on the door and ran back to stand beside Jess. "You really mean it? You'll teach us to ride?"

"If it's okay with your mom, it's okay with me," Jess assured him, once again experiencing that funny feeling in his chest when a brilliant smile broke out on the boy's freckled face.

"Hot damn!" Chad exclaimed, jumping up and down with excitement. "This is so great!"

Jess grimaced, recalling his recent assessment of the abundantly endowed Miss July who graced the calendar hanging on the back wall of the tack room. At the time, he hadn't realized that anyone else had been close to hear him compliment the shapely lady, but obviously that old adage about little pitchers having big ears was true. Since Chad took such relish in repeating every damned...darned thing he had to say, he really did have to start watching his mouth.

At the same time as that realization occurred to him. Jess came to another conclusion. Like it or not, as long as these bright-eyed, sharp-eared, rambunctious little guys lived under his roof, he wasn't just obliged to clean up his language. If he wanted to continue thinking of himself as a man of high moral principle, he had to start acting like one, set a much better example for them than he'd been setting up until now.

Okay, so he didn't care much for their mother, but it wasn't fair to take his feelings for her out on her sons. After all, it wasn't their fault that Terry was a short-tempered, avaricious shrew with homicidal tendencies. Maybe she had acted with great malice of forethought and sent her children out on a mission to antagonize him, but the boys were just being themselves, and therefore, completely innocent of any wrongdoing.

With that rationale in mind, though he still felt distinctly uncomfortable in the role, Jess delivered his first patriarchal sounding speech. "Sorry to disappoint you, Chad, but crude language has nothing to do with being a good cowboy, and I have to apologize for making remarks like that in front of you boys."

"That's okay," Chuckie declared magnanimously, giving Jess a comforting pat on one broad shoulder. "We still like you."

Jess was taken aback by that admission. Considering his surly behavior, he knew that he didn't deserve a pat on the back, but that hadn't stopped the child from bestowing one and Jess didn't have a clue as to how to respond. Nothing in his past had prepared him to handle such an example of blind trust, but the desire to return that forgiving pat seemed almost instinctive, and without even thinking, he gave into the urge.

His action was instantly rewarded by a lopsided smile and Jess felt as if his heart were turning upside down. "I like you too, Chuck, and I really am sorry for yelling at you," he confessed awkwardly, hoping he didn't sound as deeply shaken as he felt.

"Ahh, you're just having a bad day," Chad proclaimed dismissively as he reached out and took Jess's hand. "Everybody does once in a while."

"Actually I've had quite a few bad days lately," Jess admitted, gazing down at the small hand clasped in his and wondering how in hell . . . how in heck any father could allow himself to be separated from such a great kid . . . from two such great kids. If Chad and Chuck were his sons, he would never have permitted their mother to move them so far out of his reach. Never in a million years.

On the other hand, since Terry Brubacker was their mother, Jess could easily understand why her ex-husband would appreciate the considerable number of miles between Montana and Chicago. He'd only known the woman for a couple of weeks, but he already knew enough to keep his distance. If she was still living here after a couple of months, Lord only knows what he'd be willing to do to avoid her company.

"Our mom's been having some bad days lately, too," Chad informed him, still holding Jess's hand as they walked away from Brandy's stall. "Yesterday she got so mad at the television set, she started calling it names."

Jess had no trouble imagining Terry aiming a verbal assault at some helpless inanimate object. He'd learned from painful experience that when that hair-trigger temper of hers went off, she didn't possess much self-control. That's why he'd been so taken aback by the emotionless front she'd maintained for the past few days, especially since all he'd had to do was glance at her eyes to know that she was still seething inside.

Now he understood how she'd managed to keep up that unruffled act of hers. She was taking out all her pent-up frustrations on the furniture!

"What sort of names did she call it?" he inquired with an amused chuckle.

"A big, dumb galoot and an arrogant, chauvo pig."

"Yup, that sounds like she was having a pretty bad day to me," Jess agreed, knowing very well whose picture she'd imposed on that empty screen. "Is that what she told you when you asked her about it?"

Chad shot him an anxious look. "I didn't dare ask her," he admitted in a sheepish tone, clearly worried that Jess might think him a coward.

"Wise move, Chad," Jess assured, reaching out to ruffle the boy's red hair, then hiking Chuck farther up on his shoulder as they strolled together out of the barn. "A very wise move."

As she drew back the curtain on the kitchen window and watched the laughing threesome approach the house, Terry didn't know exactly what to feel. Part of her was glad that her sons seemed to be having such a great time, but another part didn't want them associating with a man of Jess Hubbard's dubious caliber. Unfortunately, even if she detested the man, she couldn't seem to convince her sons to stay away from him. All she had to do was turn her back on the boys for a few seconds, and they were dashing out of the house in order to find him.

The first time they'd taken off on her like that she'd been about to chase after them, but Grandpa Sam had advised her against it, reminding her of what she'd been like as a child. Thinking back on those early years of her life, Terry had been forced to admit that even if her grandparents had tried pinning her down, she wouldn't have stayed pinned very long. Of course, she'd adored her Grandmother Sally, had enjoyed helping her with the household chores on occasion, but when given the choice between house and barn, she'd always chosen the barn. Just like her boys were doing now with Jess, she'd trotted behind Grandpa Sam, never so happy as when he'd asked her to help him rub down the horses or pitch hay to the livestock.

Yesterday she'd stood on the back porch and looked out at the holding pens where Jess had been giving her youngest son instructions on how to water a calf. As she'd watched a wide-eyed, giggling Chuckie struggling to hold on to a heavy wooden bucket while a newly weaned calf drank its fill, she'd remembered all the times she'd struggled with the same task, and her eyes had misted up with nostalgic tears. She'd been so happy back then, so carefree and innocent. Before she'd learned how complex and disappointing the outside world could be, she'd taken infinite pleasure in doing the most ordinary of things.

As she let the kitchen curtain swing back into place, Terry reminded herself that one of her main reasons for moving her children from the city to the country was because she wanted them to understand the joy to be found in simple pleasures. Of course, she wanted them to learn that all-important lesson. Of course, she did, even if the one to teach them wasn't herself or Grandpa Sam but a hateful, fat-headed cowboy!

Clinging to that thought, she walked over to the door, pasting a wide smile on her face as she pulled it open. "It's barely eight o'clock. Isn't it a tad early yet for lunch?" she inquired brightly, doing her best to ignore the surge of jealousy that welled up inside her when she noticed that Jess had to pry Chuckie's fingers away from his neck in order to get her son to let go of him.

"Jess says he'll give us a riding lesson if you say it's okay," Chad declared, throwing both arms around his mother's waist in the hopes of attaining her instant consent.

"That's very nice of him, I'm sure," Terry acknowledged briskly. "But I'm sure Jess has several more important things to do with his time this morning."

Before she could elaborate on that argument, however, Sam swallowed the last of his morning coffee and interrupted her with his two cents worth. "Like I always say, better late than never."

Unsure of the meaning behind that cryptic remark, Terry frowned. "What's better late than never?"

As Jess sidled over to the stove to see if there was any food left over from breakfast, Sam recalled, "You were two and a half when I set you up on your first horse, and by the time you were Chad's age, you could ride with the best of them. These boys are way behind schedule."

"I wasn't aware they were on any schedule," Terry said, glancing over at Jess who was too busy filling a plate with the biscuits and gravy that she'd saved for him to notice her suspicious expression.

"It's only a couple of months till both boys start school," Sam reminded her. "And you know what'll happen if the other kids find out they can't tell one end of a horse from the other. They'll have the daylights teased out of them. I'd say there's no time to lose. You'd best take Jess up on his kindly offer right quick. Roundup's not that far away, and once that crew of wranglers shows up, Jess won't have any free time left to spare.''

Chad was quick to pick up on the fact that he'd found a second adult ally. ''Grandpa's right, Mom. We should get started on our lessons first thing this morning.''

Realizing that her eldest had his heart set on the idea and wouldn't be persuaded otherwise, Terry agreed, although she had an entirely different plan in mind than the one being presented. ''All right, Chad, but we can't expect Jess to ignore all his other work just to give you boys riding lessons. I'll teach you both myself.''

''But you're not a cowboy!'' Chad accused, looking at her as if she'd completely lost her mind. ''You're just a mom.''

Sam's laugh earned him a censorious glare, but Terry's reply to her son's accusation was calm, a feat that she wouldn't have been able to accomplish if she'd heard even the slightest chuckle from the man still standing over by the stove. ''A mom who can ride circles around most cowboys.''

''Not Jess,'' Chad maintained stubbornly, and then, to Terry's dismay, even Chuckie, her sweet, loving baby boy, turned traitor.

''Not Jess,'' he agreed firmly, pointing out a fact that his poor ignorant mother had obviously overlooked. ''He's got silver spurs on his boots and everything.''

And if that wasn't enough to convince her, Chad listed a few more of the man's ''superior'' teaching qualifications. ''He's got a real lasso on his saddle...and a fancy belt buckle, and he can even spit tobacco.''

Terry couldn't help herself. She looked over at Jess, and just as she'd suspected, he was grinning. Her fingers itched to slap that hateful smirk off his handsome face, but even though that action would provide her with a great deal of feminine satisfaction, it wouldn't change the fact that she was outmanned and outgunned.

Grudgingly, very grudgingly, Terry withdrew from the battle. ''Okay, guys, Jess can teach you to ride, but I'm warning you right now, if this mom catches either one of you with chewing tobacco, your bottoms will be too sore to sit down on a saddle.''

Both Terry and Sam did a double take when Jess drew a glossy packet out of his breast pocket, shook out the contents in the sink, then turned on the faucet and washed the moist brown leaves down the drain. ''Your mother's right about chewing tobacco, boys,'' he announced. ''It's a filthy habit and very bad for your health. As of this moment, I'm giving it up.''

''You are?'' Sam inquired with amazement, clasping one hand protectively over the shirt pocket that contained his own supply of the evil weed.

''I am,'' Jess stated firmly. ''And so should you, Sam.''

Aware that he'd drawn the attention of all eyes, Sam deftly changed the subject. ''C'mon, boys,'' he declared quickly. ''Let's you and I go out and get Brandy saddled up whilst Jess finishes up his breakfast.''

Thirty seconds later Jess and Terry were the only ones left in the kitchen. Neither one of them was will-

ing to come right out and say what they were thinking, but they were both acutely aware that they hadn't
been alone together since that day in the north pasture. Terry didn't know how Jess felt about their last
skirmish, but she would rather be trapped in the same
room with a skunk than with him. Unfortunately she'd
never been very good at hiding her feelings and that
opinion was plain on her face.

"If you find my presence so distasteful, you can
leave anytime," Jess drawled, as he picked his plate up
off the counter and carried it over to the table.

"Leave the kitchen or the ranch?" Terry inquired,
giving his chair a wide berth as she walked around the
table and began picking up the dirty dishes and used
glasses.

Jess shrugged. "Take your pick," he suggested, but
after giving the room a quick survey, he amended,
"But I must admit, the kitchen seems to be a good
place for you. Sam and I never kept it this clean, and
unlike you, neither one of us can cook worth a
damn...a darn."

His belief that a woman's place was in the kitchen
made Terry bristle, but his compliments sounded sincere, and she found his attempt to correct his language rather sweet. She was still trying to decide
whether she was more annoyed than pleased, when
Jess tipped the scales in favor of the latter.

"I appreciate your keeping this food warm for me,"
he said. "Considering how you feel about me, that
was a mighty kind thing to do."

Anxious to prove that she could be equally fair-
minded, Terry replied, "Considering the amount of

work you do around here with next to no help, you deserve a warm breakfast.''

His blue eyes jerked up in surprise. ''Thanks,'' he said, with genuine feeling, then ruined the first truly pleasant moment they'd ever shared by allowing his gaze to wander away from her face.

Terry stood there in mutinous silence, gritting her teeth as she endured his heated perusal, but after a second or two, she realized that she didn't have much control over her own eyes. The man's blatant sensuality fascinated her, and on a purely physical level, he excited her more than any man she'd ever met. Whenever she was near him, every centimeter of her body tingled with sexual awareness, and she found herself fantasizing about him.

As usual, he was wearing a blue chambray shirt and faded jeans, the normal uniform for a working cowboy, but today, he'd added a brown leather vest to his attire. The top three buttons of his shirt were undone, and she could see his deep tan, the dark curly body hair and that shiny gold coin he always wore. Whenever he breathed, it glinted, attracting her gaze. She wondered what that coin meant to him, unaware that Jess was fully cognizant of her interest.

''I wear it for luck,'' he informed her in a tone as smooth as silk. ''And in all the years I've worn it, it's never let me down.''

The hot, hungry look in his eyes told Terry that he thought he might get lucky where she was concerned, and that arrogant male assumption brought her quickly back to her senses. Maybe she did lust after his body as much as he seemed to lust after hers, but that certainly didn't mean she was willing to hop right into his bed.

"There's always a first time," she replied with saccharine sweetness, then snatched his plate out from under his nose and dumped the remaining contents into the sink.

"Yes, there is," Jess agreed as he pushed back his chair, reaching for his Stetson as he stood up from the table. "And I can't tell you how much I'm looking forward to ours."

Terry whirled around to face him, unable to let that outrageous comment pass, but Jess wasn't striding out the door, he was standing right behind her, intimidatingly close behind her, and his unexpected presence startled her so much that her mouth dropped open.

Jess laughed softly at her astonished expression, then waited for her to regain her wits and make some attempt to push him away. When she didn't, he slid one arm around her waist and jerked her against him. "Cheer up, honey," he advised her, his expression as disturbed as her own. "I don't like feeling this way anymore than you do."

Terry understood that he was about to kiss her, and she flattened her palms against his chest but found to her horror that her arms were completely devoid of strength. The instant she felt the full length of his hard body molded to hers, her brain shut down and all she could do was surrender to the primitive needs of her own flesh. Helplessly, she angled her face toward his and parted her lips, inviting the possession of his mouth.

Jess didn't hesitate. His mouth opened over hers and he kissed her. Maybe it was because he'd dreamed about this moment far too many times, but the kiss wasn't gentle. It was wild and deep and hungry. Unbelievably, it was also returned in full measure, and Jess groaned with primal pleasure when his tongue plunged into her hot, sweet mouth and was instantly challenged by hers. The give and take was incredibly exciting, an erotic duel of wills which he fully intended to win.

Even so, it soon became clear to him that Terry was equally determined to maintain her own. Her tongue met his in a frenzied dance that took his breath away. Finally a desperate need for oxygen forced him to tear his lips away from hers.

Feeling completely disoriented, Terry took a stumbling step backward but was gratified when she finally dared to glance up at Jess's face and found the same blank confusion on his features. His pupils were dilated, his irises a deep, smoldering navy, and his breathing was ragged. To Terry's amazement, she was the one who seemed to recover first, at least she was first to recover the use of her voice.

"We're not going to do this again, Jesse Hubbard," she warned him breathlessly, shaken to the core by the depths of their passion. "Never, ever again!"

Jess stared back at her in silence for several seconds, then reached up and yanked on the brim of his Stetson, pulling it down lower over his eyes. "You are one very dangerous lady, Theresa Brubacker," he murmured thickly. "And I hope you're right."

Scowling ferociously, he strode over to the door and jerked it open. "I hope to hell you're right. Because the possibility that you're not scares me to death."

Five

Considering the way he'd slammed out the door after kissing her, Terry was surprised when Jess joined the family for lunch and showed up again at supper. Not so surprising, he'd talked little during either meal, and he'd left the house immediately after supper, saying that his stallion needed some exercise. He'd looked directly at Terry when he'd said it, and the agitated expression in his blue eyes had told her that he needed the run far more than his horse.

Suffering from some highly ambivalent feelings herself, Terry had yearned to follow his example, but unlike Jess, she couldn't just eat and run. Before she could steal any free time for herself, she felt obligated to wash all the dishes and clean up the kitchen, then supervise Chad and Chuckie while they took their baths. By the time the boys were safely into their pajamas and watching television with their great-grandfather, the sun was dipping low in the sky.

Terry noticed the long shadow her figure cast on the ground as she reached the bottom of the porch steps. The sun had already sunk behind the high roof of the cow barn, and she figured there was less than an hour of strong light left. That meant she shouldn't wander too far away from the house. Hopefully she'd come up with a few answers before it grew completely dark. Now that she knew what kissing Jess was like, and it was like nothing she'd ever experienced before, she had to decide what her next move should be.

Hands in the back pockets of her jeans, she strolled behind the house and down the narrow, pine-strewn path leading to Arrowhead Creek. The shadows were darker and the air much cooler beneath the tall fir trees, and Terry was glad that she'd remembered to wear a warm sweater. She was also grateful for the number of times she'd walked this same path in her childhood, for even when the dense undergrowth made it difficult for her to tell which direction to take, her steps never faltered.

Upon reaching the meandering creek bed, she turned upstream and walked for several more yards before locating what she'd always thought of as her "thinking rock"—a giant, flat-topped granite boulder that had probably occupied the same spot for centuries. As she climbed atop the boulder and sat with both arms clasped around her knees, she was forced to ask herself if she had any viable alternatives left where Jess was concerned. She could wish him off the property as often as she liked, but she couldn't think of any

legal way to accomplish that feat, and she'd spent
most of the day wrestling with the problem. Actually
she'd spent every minute of every day for the past
week wrestling with the problem, but the facts always
remained the same. Jess Hubbard owned fifty percent of the Triple L ranch.

So where did that leave them?

In chess, the situation would be described as a
stalemate, in checkers a draw, but she and Jess weren't
on opposite sides in some trivial board game. They
were playing this game for keeps, and this morning's
impassioned contest of wills had upped the stakes even
more. Before they'd kissed one another, the spoils of
victory might have been limited to the rightful ownership of property, but afterward, both sides of the
opposition had been aware that if Jess came out on top
in their battle, he stood to gain something far more
personal than a few thousand acres of land.

Terry couldn't afford to let that happen. Eventually she might have to accept the fact that Jess couldn't
be bought out, but if she ever expected him to treat her
as a business partner, to give her an equal voice in
running things, she absolutely could not allow him to
lay claim to her body as easily as he'd laid claim to the
ranch.

She'd lost her identity to a man once. No matter
how strongly she desired a man, she couldn't take such
a risk again. For the first time in eight years she was
the master of her own fate, and she was determined to
stay in command. Maybe she and Jess would make
love one day, she was beginning to think that might be
a foregone conclusion, but before it could happen, she

needed to set down some ground rules for the business aspects of their relationship.

Unfortunately making sure she didn't sacrifice her personal integrity just for the pleasure of a quick toss in the hay meant that she had to arrange another confrontation with Jess, and considering the combustible nature of their attraction, she wasn't too sure she could keep things on an impersonal level long enough to convince him of anything. If Jess lost control of his temper over something she said and he kissed her again with such devastating thoroughness, Terry feared that she might lie down and surrender without even so much as a whimper.

"And then where would I be?" she muttered under her breath, very much aware that her time was swiftly running out. Somehow she had to break their impasse, and she had to do it soon. But how?

Terry scowled as a highly repugnant word pushed itself to the forefront of her mind and refused to be ignored. Compromise.

For the sake of her marriage to Doug, she'd made enough concessions to last her a lifetime, which was why she absolutely hated the idea of conceding anything to an arrogant male chauvinist like Jess. Yet, what other choice did she really have? He'd made it very plain that he wouldn't sell out to her. She could rant and rave and carry on about it for all she was worth, but Jess Hubbard still wouldn't budge on that issue.

Therefore, until such time as it suited him to move on, she was well and truly stuck with him, and the only thing left for her to do was make the best of it. For her part, making the best of it meant that she should have as much say as Jess in all future decisions concerning the ranch. No matter what he said, Jess was a drifter, and sooner or later he was going to lose interest in the Triple L. When he got itchy feet and decided to take off in search of a bigger and better challenge, she didn't want to be left in an ignorant position.

Consequently it was imperative that she be involved in the day-to-day operations, be advised of every change Jess was contemplating, and agree to it. Her okay should appear on every check written off the ranch account. After all, Jess couldn't possibly deny that she had a vested interest in the place, even if her investment wasn't as large as his. Of course, knowing how he thought, if she expected him to account to her for his expenditures, he would tell her exactly what she could do with her money.

Frustrated by that possibility, Terry picked up a small pebble and threw it into the shallow waters of the creek bed. She stood a better chance of convincing a grizzly bear to come out of hibernation in early December than convincing Boss Man Hubbard to agree to her terms, and the grizzly's response to her action would likely be ten times more pleasant.

"So, how would you bring up such a tricky subject to such a touchy man?" she asked an unsuspecting raccoon that had come to the creek for a drink, not surprised when the alarmed animal darted away on its short, fat legs and dived into the underbrush.

Nodding her head at the frightened creature, Terry declared, "My sentiments exactly."

"Since running away from me won't do you any good, I suggest you give the head-on approach a try."

Terry gasped and swiveled around on her granite perch. Jess was leaning against a nearby pine tree, one knee bent, the heel of his boot resting against the trunk. He was grinning at her, highly amused to find her talking about him to a raccoon.

Aware that she'd just confirmed herself as a total ditz in his eyes, Terry wanted to scream in exasperation, but all she offered was a weak question. "What are you doing here?"

Tipping his hat to the back of his head, Jess let his gaze run over her flushed face, the slimness of her neck, and the rise and fall of her full breasts, leaving her with the sensation that he had touched her.

When he spoke to her again, he was no longer smiling. "If you have something that important to discuss with me, you'd better start talking now, before it starts raining."

"Raining?" Even as she asked the question, Terry heard a distant rumble of thunder.

"We're in for a storm." Jess pointed his thumb over his left shoulder to a break in the trees where Terry could see the horizon and the solid shadow of clouds rising up over the top of the mountains. "That's why I came after you. Apparently Sam was right to think you might not notice."

Terry sniffed disdainfully. "You needn't have troubled yourself. A little rain won't hurt me."

Jess cocked his head towards the rolling black storm cloud. "Since you've been away from the ranch so long, you must have forgotten what storms are like in this part of the country," he declared scornfully. "That monster is rolling in over the mountains, and when the wind comes off those upper elevations, the temperature is going to drop fast. Get drenched and you could wind up with pneumonia."

Another ominous rumble could be heard, still in the distance but definitely moving closer, and when Terry put that sound together with the cold breeze that whipped suddenly across her face, she jumped down from the boulder without any further argument. "At the rate those clouds are moving, we're both going to get wet."

Jess didn't appear to be too worried about that possibility. Then he whistled through his teeth, and Terry found out why. Answering his master's summons, Dusty stepped out from between two trees. In the blink of an eye, Jess was mounted on the stallion's broad back and holding his hand out to Terry. "Coming?"

A flash of lightning zigzagged across the patch of open sky overhead, and Terry didn't need to be asked twice. Astonishing Jess with her agility, she sprinted toward his outstretched arm. Upon reaching it, she clasped both of her hands around his elbow, then swung herself up into the saddle behind him.

"That was a neat trick," he acknowledged slowly, reluctant to believe that the difficult stunt she'd just pulled had been anything more than a fluke. Then again, maybe it wasn't, and if that was the case, she hadn't been trying to murder him the other day in the north pasture. "Did you ever compete as a stunt rider?"

"I won an award at our local rodeo for barrel racing when I was fourteen," Terry informed him. "But I never did any trick riding, at least not in public. I only pretended to be Annie Oakley when I was home. Actually," she recalled with a chuckle, "Grandpa Sam blames me for every white hair on his head."

As he laced the reins through his fingers, Jess tried to imagine her as a young girl, amazed by how easy it was for him to picture her as a teenage daredevil. Dark eyes sparkling with excitement, silky black hair flying out behind her, he could see her jumping up on the back of a horse, scaring Sam almost to death as she attempted some balancing act.

Recalling that Annie Oakley was an expert at something else besides bareback riding, he inquired, "Does that mean you're an excellent markswoman as well?"

Delighted by the wariness in his tone, Terry warned cheekily, "I can hold my own with a rifle."

"Wonderful," Jess grumbled under his breath, and when the woman behind him giggled in his ear, he jerked on Dusty's reins.

"Walking might be faster," Terry observed, gazing back over her shoulder at the slippery rocks strewn along the creek bed and the steep slopes rising up on either side of the gully. "A horse can't negotiate very well over this kind of terrain."

"Just hang on," Jess advised her grimly, taking one last glance at the darkening sky before he dug a heel into Dusty's flank. The horse needed no further urging but bounded into the shallow water of the stream and broke into an unsteady canter. Terry wrapped both arms around Jess's waist and held on for dear life.

"I thought the purpose of this ride was to stay dry." Terry complained through clenched teeth, pressing her face tightly against Jess's back as the stallion's pounding hooves kicked up a steady spray of moisture.

Jess didn't respond to her complaint, nor direct his horse to lessen speed. As the first droplet of cold rain fell from the sky, he jerked hard on the reins, and the stallion complied with the command by careening off to the left and plunging through a narrow passage between the trees. A few seconds later Dusty carried them onto a flat section of open ground.

As soon as he felt the level terrain under his hooves, the horse broke into a gallop, trying valiantly to outrun the clouds that were rapidly taking over the sky. The try was in vain. Thunder clapped behind the clouds, lightning flashed, and as if on cue, the heavens opened up.

Terry gasped in shock as the frigid deluge poured down on her bare head, nearly blinding her. One flash of lightning was instantly followed by another and another, until the air around them seemed alive with electricity. More frightened than she cared to admit, Terry tightened her hold on Jess and started praying.

Less willing to rely on Divine intervention, Jess shouted to be heard above the thunder. "It's an electrical storm. We're going to have to take cover!" As he turned his head, a torrent of water whipped off the brim of his Stetson. "That way!"

On command, Dusty took off down a narrow, treeless corridor that Terry recognized as the old logging road, "No, Jess!" she screamed frantically. "This old road won't take us anywhere!"

As usual, Jess paid absolutely no attention to her warning. As thunder rumbled and vibrated the earth around them, he urged the stallion to run faster, then faster yet. Lighting danced across the sky and bolted between the tops of tall trees. Terry squeezed her eyes shut and prayed like she had never prayed before.

Miraculously, in a matter of moments, her prayers were answered. Dusty stopped running, the rain stopped pounding down on her head, and the cold wind stopped trying to drag her shivering body out of the saddle. Cautiously, Terry opened one eye, amazed when she discovered that she hadn't been transported to some heavenly shelter.

When she swept her dripping hair off her forehead, she could see that they were in some kind of a cave, a deep recess carved into the foundation of a sandstone cliff. Terry had always assumed that as a child, she'd either walked or ridden over every square inch of Triple L land, but this was one spot she'd missed. Since Jess had ridden right to the place, Terry had to acknowledge that maybe, just maybe, he knew a bit more about the ranch than she'd been willing to give him credit for.

"I never knew this cave was here," she admitted wonderingly, gazing up at the vaulted ceiling and smooth sandstone walls. "And I've ridden up and down that logging road a hundred times."

"You can't see this cliff from the road," Jess told her, as he assisted her to the ground, then dismounted himself.

"Then how did you manage to find it?"

Jess's expression was decidedly sheepish, which made Terry even more curious. "Jess?" she persisted, sensing his reluctance to answer.

He pulled off his hat, shook the water off onto the ground, then lifted his hand and raked his fingers through his damp hair. "Okay, so I was out chasing a really dumb stray calf and got caught in a storm just like this one," he admitted grudgingly.

"And?"

"And I ended up here."

Terry studied his closed expression for a few seconds, then cocked her head to one side and inquired, "So what's the rest of the story?"

Jess emitted a long-suffering sigh. "So that damn calf had been leading me to hell and gone all day long, but when the rains came, she led me straight to this shelter, which made me wonder which one of us was really the stupid one."

Terry bit her lower lip to keep from laughing, recalling what had happened to her the last time she'd laughed at him, but then she noted the self-derisive glint of humor in his eyes, and her laughter burst free.

Jess waited, certain that she wouldn't be able to resist making some kind of smart remark about his intelligence, but when she finally stopped giggling and glanced over at him, she shook her head. "Uh-uh, I wouldn't touch that comment with a lodgepole pine."

Jess tied Dusty's reins to a stubby bush near the entrance to the cave, then turned back to face her, the damp, blond curls clinging to his forehead making him look more boyish than Terry had ever seen him. "I'm much obliged."

Terry smiled, pleased by the sudden sense of camaraderie that existed between them. When Jess bent down and started picking up the dead twigs and broken tree branches that were scattered inside the wide entrance to the cave, she pitched in to help without being asked. "I hope you brought some matches," she said, once her arms were full of kindling. "Because all I've got in my pockets are a couple of sticks of gum."

"A good scout is always prepared," Jess replied as he dumped his load of dry wood onto the ground, then hunkered down beside a circle of stones that Terry hadn't noticed before.

"Just how long were you and that stupid calf trapped in here?" she inquired, noticing that the stone circle already contained several inches of burnt ash.

"Long enough to become the best of buddies," Jess admitted with a wry grin.

Terry smiled, wondering if the two of them would be so lucky. "How long do you think this storm will last?"

"It's too violent to keep up for very long," Jess said, then pointed to a wide outcropping of stone in the wall of the cave. "You might as well sit down over there and make yourself comfortable while I get this fire started."

Terry walked over to the wide rock shelf and sat down, shivering as a blast of cold wind blew through the entrance. She wrapped her arms around her chest but found no warmth in the action. Her sweater was a sodden mass of wet wool, the blouse beneath it damp and rapidly growing damper. The fire would likely take the edge off the cold, but it would be hours before it was warm enough inside the cave to start drying their clothes.

"Did you happen to bring an extra saddle blanket with you?" she inquired, as soon as Jess had a small blaze going. "I'm freezing and I'd like to take off this sweater before I'm totally wet to the skin."

Jess's head came around, and he stared at her, his blue eyes igniting with heat as they focused on her breasts. "You want to take off your sweater?" he repeated stupidly.

Recognizing that intense look, Terry stiffened her spine. "I'm not planning to do a striptease, if that's what you're wondering."

The hateful grin that Terry thoroughly despised was in place on his face, as Jess drawled, "Too bad. That would've been an enjoyable way to pass the time."

Terry sat motionless, totally disheartened. "Why did you have to go and spoil everything?" she demanded tightly. "We were finally getting along, behaving like friends, and then you had to say something like that."

Jess was standing at the entrance to the cave, hands jammed into the back pockets of his jeans as he gazed out at the brilliant surges of lightning. For a moment Terry feared he wasn't going to answer her, but then he turned around to face her and she feared that he would. His savage expression matched the one he'd worn this morning when he'd called her a dangerous lady. "You know damned well that you have this power to arouse me," he ground out harshly.

Terry lowered her eyes. "Yes," she murmured helplessly.

"So why should it bother you to hear me say it?"

Hearing him say that he wanted her did bother her, but it wasn't what bothered her the most. It was wanting him so much that she could barely see straight. His suggestive words had inspired a frenzy of other unwanted feelings as well. She felt excited, confused, and angry all at the same time. He'd deliberately provoked her, but even knowing that, the turbulent, elemental tension inside her refused to abate.

"Nothing you say bothers me," she lied.

"No?"

"No!"

When Jess started toward her, Terry's heart started pounding, and by the time he stood towering over her, her breathing pattern was totally erratic. "We barely know each other," she choked out in desperation, the determined glint in his eyes igniting a scorching heat that licked through her veins. "And what we do know, we don't like."

"When it comes to this, it doesn't matter what else we know," Jess insisted, placing both hands on her shoulders as he lifted her up to stand before him. "Or like."

Terry felt his warm hand on the small of her back, arching her into the ever tightening circle of his arms. Thunder rocked the ground beneath her feet, but she couldn't tell the difference between it and the tremors of desire that shuddered through her body. "Please, Jess," she begged, shivering uncontrollably. "Don't do this . . . not before we get a few things settled."

"What else is there to settle?"

"The cattle business . . . our partnership," she stammered breathlessly, unable to look anywhere but at his hard mouth. "We . . . we really have to talk about the future."

"Do we?" he inquired seductively, smiling at the betraying heat that scorched her cheeks. Terry licked her dry lips, unaware that the sight of her small, pink tongue ruined any chance of further conversation.

"Yes, we do," she insisted, but her words ended in a soft moan of pleasure as his head descended.

Jess covered her protesting lips with his mouth. It was a violent kiss, the primal kind that awakened an urgent desire in a woman to mate with the man who was claiming her. Terry trembled at the strength of that basic need, which could make her lips yield so willingly to his mouth, her body fit itself so eagerly to every indent and plane of his masculine frame. The feel of his hips moving against hers evoked a response from her that was as ravishing and seductive as the final act itself.

Jess slid his hands much lower on her back, pulling her into the cradle of his thighs. With one hand pressed to the base of her spine, he held her in the exact place that he wanted. Terry needed no encouragement to meet his sensual challenge. She arched her back, molded her lower body to his unyielding hardness, and matched his tormenting ardor, kiss for kiss.

Jess knew Terry couldn't deny her response, but he didn't disengage himself from their sensual duel until he was sure that she was aware of her own helplessness, the impossibility of rejecting what had been started the first moment they'd set eyes on one another. Unfortunately, bringing home that point to her was sheer torture for him, the need to be inside her all-consuming.

He couldn't take her, not here, but maybe, before he was forced to pull himself up short, he could enjoy a bit more of what she was willing to offer. Maybe she'd allow him to caress her lush breasts, to cup her fullness in his hands, to draw a nipple into his mouth and savor the wild taste of her. Maybe she'd even encourage him to bare her completely.

Even as he thought it, Jess felt Terry's hands moving over him, her fingers sliding between the buttons of his wet shirt to the hot, damp skin beneath, proving that she wanted to touch him, needed to touch him. Groaning with pleasure, Jess lifted his mouth away from hers and took a fraction of a step backward, making space for his hand to pull the material of his shirt free from its buttons.

Terry lowered her head to his broad chest, her teeth grazing one nipple as her fingers caressed and explored him. Jess shuddered violently against her, as if she'd just breached some barrier that he'd sought to keep erect. Somewhat fearfully, she realized that such a breach would demand instant retaliation, and she barely had time for a quick intake of breath before he pulled up her sweater and slid his hand beneath her blouse. As his hot, searching fingers seared through the fragile lace of her bra, Terry moaned, needing all barriers to be gone.

A second later Jess drew her wet sweater up over her head, then removed her blouse and bra and tossed all three over his shoulder. Then he was dragging her to the ground as if he were caught in an undertow that not even he, with all his powerful muscles and dynamic strength, could withstand. Terry understood what he was feeling for she was trapped in the same riptide of desire, drowning in wondrous sensations.

The irresistible longings had her writhing and twisting beneath him as his mouth sought the dusty rose tip of her breast. Her fingers spread over his bare chest, her body savoring the feel of his fiery skin against her own. He murmured her name as he moved his mouth against her throat, her ear, her cheek, and finally her lips. His weight pressed her slim body onto the hard ground.

He was reaching for the snap on her jeans when lightning split open the sky in front of the cavern. Dusty neighed in alarm and strained against the tied reins. Rearing his hooves, the stallion danced backward, his hind legs coming dangerously close to the entwined pair on the ground.

Reacting with pantherlike reflexes, Jess rolled Terry out of reach of the trampling hooves and continued the fluid motion until he was on his feet. "Easy, boy." His husky voice attempted to quiet his horse. "Easy now."

Shaking with reaction, Terry searched frantically for her blouse and bra. Finding them, she stuffed her bra into the pocket of her jeans, then pushed her arms through the sleeves of her blouse, but her fingers were trembling too badly to fasten the buttons. Completing that simple task seemed to take her forever, and it took an eternity longer before she felt steady enough to stand up.

Jess caught her movement out of the corner of his eye. He gave Dusty a last reassuring pat, retied the reins, and walked back to her. Even though his eyes still smoldered with frustrated passion, he made no move to take up where they'd left off. A muscle twitched in his jaw as he growled, "You wanted me as much as I wanted you."

Troubled confusion shimmered in her eyes, but Terry's reply was clear. "Yes, I did."

Jess nodded, his expression strangely satisfied. "Good," he declared tersely. "I'll expect you to keep that fact in mind when we have that talk about our future because that's how it's going to be from now on."

Six

"That's how what's going to be?" Terry inquired tightly, not too sure what Jess was trying to tell her but quite certain she didn't like his autocratic tone.

"Our relationship," Jess retorted, his eyes daring her to deny what had almost happened between them, what would have happened if Dusty hadn't gotten spooked. "Our partnership, or association, or whatever else you want to call it."

"What would you call it?" Terry wanted to know, still not positive she was understanding him correctly.

Jess appeared to give that question serious thought, before he shrugged his bare shoulders carelessly. "For lack of any better term, I'd call it an affair."

"An affair," Terry repeated speculatively, as if she were testing out that possibility in her mind, as if she didn't despise that particular word with every single bone in her body. In her opinion, an affair was something one married partner did behind the back of the other, and neither she nor Jess was married. Whatever they were involved in, it wasn't an affair. An affair was something that broke hearts, shattered all trust, and made a mockery of solemn promises. Affairs wounded innocent children, destroyed families, and turned warm, caring women into cold, mistrustful cynics.

"Oh, no, I won't ever have an affair," Terry vowed, very much aware that she was one woman, who as a result of her ex-husband's betrayal, might not ever dare to risk her heart in the same way again.

Immersed in her own private torment, Terry didn't realize that she'd spoken out loud until Jess started railing at her. "How can you stand there and say that to me after what just happened between us? Do you think I'm an idiot!"

Terry's eyes widened in alarm when Jess stalked toward her. "Of course not!"

"Then why are you denying the truth?" he demanded angrily, grabbing hold of her wrist when she would've backed away. "Maybe you need a more graphic demonstration than the one I just gave you before you'll admit what's happening between us?"

Terry flushed at his words. The erotic picture they created in her mind heated her blood, and she could feel the sensual flames spreading like wildfire through her veins. "I'm very well aware of what's happening," she countered resentfully. "You don't have to hit me over the head with it."

Jess had a dangerous look in his eyes. "That's your real problem, isn't it? You consider yourself too much of a lady to lust after a rude, crude cowboy like me!"

Terry tried to jerk her arm free from his hold, but his grip was like steel. "I didn't say any such thing," she finally exclaimed, more out of frustration than fear. For in truth, as large as this man was, as intimidating as he could be at times, like now, nothing he said or did had ever truly scared her. Excited her, yes…angered her? Definitely, but somehow she knew that Jess would never actually hurt her, at least not physically.

From what he'd just said, however, Terry realized that she wasn't the only one who'd suffered through a bad relationship with a member of the opposite sex. Amazing as it seemed to her, considering how self-contained and confident he always seemed to be, she'd just discovered that Jess wasn't entirely invulnerable. At some point in his past, he'd been rejected too, apparently because the woman he wanted hadn't considered him good enough for her. But Terry's fear of involvement with him had nothing to do with his supposedly rough manners and unacceptable social status.

Sighing, Terry murmured, "I don't deny that I want you, Jess. How could I?"

Jess frowned at her unhappy tone, sensing there was something else behind her refusal to call a spade a spade than some hypocritical notion that she was too good for him. If he were honest, he'd have to admit that due to his past experience with women, he was overly sensitive in that area. Therefore, wasn't it just as possible that due to her past experience with men, Terry might also be supersensitive about a few things? Have a healthy mistrust of his sex? "But you wish you could deny it, don't you?"

"Yes, I do," she admitted honestly, then offered him a rueful smile. "For all the good that kind of wishful thinking does me."

"Tell me about it," Jess growled, then let go of her wrist. Trying to regain his lost calm, he closed his eyes for a few seconds. When he opened them again, Terry was still standing in the same spot, looking up at him, the pained expression on her face matching his feelings.

"So what do you want to do about it?" he asked wearily. "Pretend our attraction doesn't exist?"

"Do you think that would work?"

"Nope."

Terry sighed. "Me neither."

"So?"

"So why don't we work on the other aspects of our relationship that have nothing to do with sex," Terry suggested tentatively, moving closer to the fire as she began to shiver. "It might help to keep our minds off it."

Jess became aware of the cold at the same time as she did and went to retrieve the blanket she'd requested earlier. On his way over to Dusty, he picked up his shirt and pulled it on, but it was still wet and provided very little warmth. When he came back with the blanket, Terry was sitting on the ground, as close to the fire as she could get.

"The rain's stopping," he said, as he dropped the blanket over her hunched shoulders. "If you don't mind getting a little wetter, we could leave right now and continue this conversation in a much warmer setting."

Terry looked up at him in astonishment. "You're still talking to me!"

Jess lifted one brow at that unexpected query. "Shouldn't I be?"

"Well, you didn't exactly embrace my suggestion with open arms. When you turned your back on me like that, I assumed you were angry."

"Frustrated, maybe," Jess admitted. "But not angry."

"So you're willing to hear out my plan?"

Jess appeared far less eager than he sounded. "By all means. I can't wait to hear your ideas for keeping my filthy mind off sex."

"Our minds," Terry amended, her prim, schoolmarmish tone in such total conflict with what she'd just said that Jess had to laugh.

"Sorry, ma'am," he returned smartly. "I stand corrected. Your mind is equally filthy."

If he thought she was going to take umbrage with that remark, he was dead wrong. The hurt in his voice when he'd assumed that she didn't want him because of who he was had been very real, and Terry wanted him to know that unlike whomever had rejected him, she didn't judge men by their occupation. Standing up, she poked one arm out from beneath the blanket and waggled a finger at him.

"And don't you ever forget it," she directed him sternly.

On the ride back to the ranch Terry made it impossible for Jess to think about anything else. With her arms wrapped around his waist and her full breasts pressed tightly against his back, he could feel the twin points of her nipples poking into him. Since he was seated first in the saddle, his body shielded hers from the full force of the frigid wind, but that protection surely didn't account for the amount of heat he felt searing through the back of his shirt. In order to be that warm Terry had to be thinking some very hot thoughts, and trying to imagine what they were generated so much heat inside Jess that he barely felt the wind himself.

By the time they reached the barn, he was so fully aroused that he didn't dare dismount, fearing that he might unman himself on the saddlehorn if he made the attempt. Hoping his deference to her came off as polite, Jess swiveled around from the waist and offered Terry his hand, urging her to dismount first. "I'll take care of Dusty. You run up to the house and tell Sam that you're okay. He's sure to be waiting up for you."

"I don't expect he was too worried," Terry said, ignoring Jess's offer of assistance as she propped the weight of her torso on both palms, pushed down with her arms, and sprung backward off the stallion's hindquarters. "But I bet my boys are nearly beside themselves."

Amazed by another of her nimble stunts, Jess shook his head in admiration as he responded to her last comment. "I told the boys to go to bed before I rode out to find you."

Terry's brows went up. "And they obeyed you, just like that?"

Jess grinned at her incredulity. "Sure, after I reminded them that good cowboys always follow their ramrod's orders."

"Of course," Terry muttered, not nearly so willing to accept his authority as her sons and completely oblivious to the fact that she was acting under similar orders herself as she walked out of the barn and started off for the house.

It was almost a half hour later when Jess followed her. Upon entering the kitchen, he discovered that the rest of the downstairs lights had been shut off, but he wasn't that surprised. He hadn't really expected her to be there, waiting up for him, though he was disappointed to learn that she was perfectly capable of talking out of both sides of her mouth.

Actually he wasn't just disappointed but angry, Jess realized, angry with himself for being so gullible where she was concerned. Terry wasn't different. She was just like every other woman he'd known, even if she did come in a terrific looking package that any man would ache to unwrap. Beneath that tempting outside layer, she was just as self-serving, devious, and deceitful as most other members of her sex.

Obviously her urgent need to talk about their future had diminished fast once she'd gotten safely out of his villainous clutches. All those disarming comments she'd made about desiring him had been just that, a clever ploy to keep him disarmed and, therefore, at bay. Deciding that he needed a hot shower and a pair of dry underwear much more than a meaningless conversation with a treacherous woman who didn't have the guts to confront her own feelings, Jess strode down the center hall toward the front stairs, stripping his damp shirt off along the way.

For a while there tonight, he'd been willing to give her the benefit of the doubt, especially when she'd come right out and admitted that her thoughts about him weren't exactly pure. Fool that he was, he'd admired her effort to be honest with him, but now he realized that, like most other women when it came to admitting their lust, she was a narrow-minded prude. Once the aftereffects of their passion had worn off, she'd been ashamed of her wanton surrender, and she certainly hadn't wanted to sit down with him and listen to a rehash of her downfall.

As he passed by the wide arched entry to the front room, Jess wondered what Terry could possibly tell herself that would place him in the role of evil seducer and her as an innocent victim. Of course, if she were as adept at lying to herself as the other women he'd known, she'd somehow manage to convince herself that she'd done her level best to fight him off.

"I've got a fire started, and I've made us a pot of decaffeinated coffee. Do you want a cup now, or would you rather wait and drink it after you've changed out of those damp clothes?"

"Huh!" Jess dropped his shirt as he whirled around, his startled gaze jumping from the small, cheery fire that was burning in the fireplace to the tall, slender woman in the full-length, faded, blue flannel bathrobe who was curled up on the couch, calmly sipping her coffee. She'd pulled up her hair into a haphazard topknot, and the loose tendrils framing her face gave her a tousled look that Jess found incredibly sexy.

It took several seconds for him to recover his poise, and even then his voice sounded hoarse. "You didn't tell me this was going to be a pajama party."

Terry wrinkled her nose in disapproval, frowning at him as if he were a naughty boy, and a great trial to a woman's patience. "I'm wearing this old robe because it's warm and comfortable and because I didn't have enough energy when I got out of the shower to button a blouse and pull on another pair of jeans."

Jess swallowed hard. "You mean all you're wearing is that robe!"

Terry took a deep breath and silently counted to ten, a trick that she often used when one of her sons severely taxed her temper. "If you really must know," she finally declared through tight lips. "This ultra-sexy robe comes with a matching nightgown that's guaranteed to drive a man wild. It has an enticing rip in the hem, twelve strategically placed buttons starting at the chin, and an extremely erotic looking coffee stain down the front. Would you like me to model it for you?"

By the end of her description, Jess felt like a prize fool. "That won't be necessary," he mumbled, as he bent down to pick up his shirt. "I got the message."

"Good," Terry retorted, smiling in satisfaction when Jess retreated sheepishly up the stairs.

He was back less than ten minutes later, wearing mismatched cotton socks, a baggy pair of gray sweatpants, and a ratty looking navy blue T-shirt which was stretched out around the neck and sported a ragged tear in the side seam. His blond hair was more wet than damp from what had to be one of the fastest showers on record, but the stubborn curl he'd vainly attempted to slick down on his head was already threatening to spring back over his brow.

Clasping one hand over her heart, Terry fluttered her lashes at him and declared, "Be still, my heart."

Jess grinned, admiring her sense of humor and her appreciation of his outfit. "That's what all the women say when they see me in this sexy getup," he informed her, then picked up a mug off the tray and poured himself some coffee. "Do you think you can keep your hands off me while we talk?"

"It'll be tough," Terry conceded dryly. "But I'll try to manage."

"And I'll do the same," Jess declared sincerely, and in that moment, Terry realized that she could end up really liking this man, as well as desiring him. Of course, that realization only intensified the problem they were facing. If they somehow managed to combine friendship with desire, how long would it be before another, far more damaging emotion followed?

Apparently Jess was thinking along those same lines. "Do you think it's possible for us to be friends?"

"If we want this ranch to succeed, I think we have to try," Terry replied softly, trying to quell her body's instant response when Jess sat down next to her, slid one tanned arm along the top of the couch behind her shoulders, stretched out his long, muscular legs, and propped his stocking feet up on the coffee table.

"Okay," Jess agreed companionably. "Then let me start by apologizing to you for the way I turned down your offer to buy me out. I should've been much more tactful."

"And I shouldn't have reacted so violently," Terry conceded. "I was only trying to scare you. I wouldn't have actually trampled you to death."

"Well, that's a positive step forward, don't you think?"

Terry returned his smile, took another sip of her coffee, then rested her head back on the sofa cushion. "From now on, murder threats are out."

Aware that she was starting to relax in his company, Jess thought better of asking her how she felt about a different sort of bodily threat, but being so close to her like this in what might be considered a highly romantic setting provoked some mighty tempting thoughts. "And I'll stop making cracks about your being a prissy, know-nothing, city woman looking out for the main chance. I was wrong on both counts."

Terry was relieved that he no longer thought of her as greedy, but this was the first time she'd heard that he also considered her a prissy know-nothing. "I don't see how you could've thought that in the first place!" she exclaimed indignantly. "Surely Grandpa Sam told you that while I was growing up, I worked as long and hard as any other ranch hand."

"No, he didn't," Jess said. "I was kept as much in the dark about you as you were about me. In fact, up until the day he told me that you'd bought a quarter share of the ranch, I wasn't aware that Sam had any family. Not only that, but considering his outspoken opinions about the weaker sex, I couldn't believe that he'd actually take on a female partner.''

Terry rolled her eyes heavenward, well aware of her grandfather's archaic viewpoint concerning her gender. Even during her late teens when she'd worked side by side with him, proving that she could do most anything a man could do, Grandpa Sam had stubbornly held on to the opinion that a woman's place was in the home. "I don't doubt that," she conceded bitterly. "And unfortunately he still believes that it's a woman's lot in life to be a wife and a mother. He simply refuses to accept the fact that I could run this place just fine without a man's help."

"Which is where I come in," Jess stated grimly.

Terry nodded. "I'm afraid so, but that's Sam's perception, not mine. I have no intention of spending all my time cooking meals and cleaning house while the two of you decide what's best for the Triple L. I made the mistake of limiting myself to a domestic role during my marriage, but never again."

Eyes narrowed with suspicion, Jess demanded. "Speaking of your marriage, exactly how long ago was it that you and uh . . ."

"Douglas."

"Yeah, that you and Douglas decided on a divorce?" Jess inquired. "And when did you inform Sam?"

Terry's thoughts went back to that terrible day when she'd been forced to give up on the delusion that her marriage could be saved. When she'd discovered that her husband was having an affair with one of the other lawyers in his firm, a glamorous, sophisticated career woman who adored spending money on herself and abhorred the idea of being anyone's mother, Terry had accepted that it was the end. Doug had forgotten his briefcase when he'd left home that morning, and dutiful wife that she'd been, Terry had brought it over to him. Assuming that Doug's secretary had stepped out for a few minutes, she'd entered his office unannounced and thereby discovered her less than loving husband making love to someone else.

From that moment, their marriage had been over. Terry had contacted a lawyer that very afternoon, and though that devastating phone call was still very clear in her mind, she couldn't recall the exact time she'd passed on the news to Grandpa Sam. "Let's see...the divorce was final on the second of January, and we were legally separated for six months before that, so I'd say Grandpa Sam has known about my breakup with Doug for a little over a year."

"And when did he start badgering you to move yourself and the kids back here to the ranch?"

"Right after he forced it out of me that Doug was having an affair," Terry admitted, hoping that revelation would foster a deeper understanding between her and Jess. Now that he knew what had prompted her to seek a divorce, surely he would comprehend why she'd reacted so vehemently to his suggestion that they were having an affair.

Maybe Jess would've responded sympathetically to Terry's admission if he hadn't been struck by an en-

tirely different kind of revelation. "Jeezus, Mary, and
Martha!" he swore, outraged fury in his eyes as he
realized the full extent of Sam Lawson's perfidy. "I
was set up right from the start! That's why he stalled
so long before signing the final sales papers. Dammit
to hell, that . . . that conniving old coot was testing me
out, trying to decide if I was the right candidate for the
job!"

Terry stared at him in utter astonishment, staggered by the waves of hostility radiating from him.
"Jess?"

"Sweet, bloody hell! I sold my soul to the devil
himself!"

"What on earth are you talking about?"

Jess jerked his head around, intending to accuse her
of being a willing accomplice in the lousiest, most un-
derhanded scheme he'd ever heard of in his life, but
the total lack of comprehension on her face convinced him that she was an innocent victim. "You
really don't know, do you?"

"Know what?" Terry exclaimed in exasperation.

"That I'm your grandfather's handpicked choice to
be your next husband and Chad and Chuck's new
daddy?"

"What!"

Ten minutes later Jess had effectively convinced her
that his supposition was correct, and Terry was still
reeling from the shock, but beyond that she was mor-
tified. To secure his idea of a proper husband for her,
Grandpa Sam had actually gone and sold half of the
Triple L. According to Jess, the financial problems

facing the ranch were very real, but that hadn't been Sam's prime motivation in choosing a buyer.

A few weeks after the sale had been made final, Jess had learned that a land developer had offered Sam far more money than he had, but Sam had turned that offer down flat. When Jess had asked why, the older man had told him that preserving a time-honored life-style was far more important to him than making a huge profit. He never had been interested in selling outright. Eventually, if he hadn't found the right partner, he would've been forced to auction off his stock and machinery, but Jess had showed up in the nick of time.

It was Sam's contention that even if he and Jess had to scrape by on next to no profit for several more years, the Triple L would still be one of the few places left on earth where a man was always king of his own castle. On a cattle ranch, even one that wasn't making much money, a man could live by his own rules, raise his sons up to be "real" men. As soon as Sam had learned that Jess shared a similarly old-fashioned and sentimental viewpoint, he'd promptly agreed to the sale.

"One of Grandpa's biggest complaints about Doug was that he was making the boys into sissies," Terry groused in vexation. "I'm sure that's why he didn't let me stop them from following you around every minute of the day. Big tough, macho man that he thinks you are, he's hoping your ways will rub off on them."

"Sam's the one who sicced those two on me!" Jess exclaimed incredulously.

His tone made it sound as if he'd been set upon by rabid dogs, and Terry cast him a baleful look. "This from the man who's supposedly going to make them a perfect father?"

Jess winced at her sarcasm. "Hey!" he reminded her. "That's Sam's perception, not mine. I know next to nothing about kids, and to tell you the truth, I'm not that sure I want to learn."

"I appreciate your honesty," Terry replied. "Though I doubt your feelings about children make any real difference to Grandpa Sam. As far as he's concerned, any man who can ride a horse and hold his own in a barroom brawl would make a dandy father."

"Unfortunately I have to agree with you," Jess said. "And that makes me wonder what qualifications he thinks I possess that will make me a great husband."

It was obvious that Jess still didn't comprehend how her grandfather thought, but Terry understood why such a thoroughly detestable scheme would make perfect sense to him. In Sam's estimation, any cowboy would make a better father for her boys than Doug Brubacker, but the old man's scheming had taken into account several other factors besides that one. Upon his death, Terry would inherit the ranch, but he didn't trust her, a mere woman, to operate it successfully. He believed that a woman couldn't survive in the world without a man's help and support. In Sam's opinion, if she married a strong, hardworking man like Jess, all of her future problems would be solved.

"I think I can make a good guess," she confessed, as her resentful gaze slid over his tall, muscular body, her eyes lingering for one pointed second at the noticeable swelling between his thighs. "And so can you," she suggested in a withering tone, then turned her bleak gaze toward the fireplace.

Jess slumped back on the couch, emulating Terry's morose posture. Like her, he stared unseeingly into the flames. He despised the notion that Sam might have taken his stud value into account when making the decision to bring him on as a partner, but Terry was convinced of it, and he had no reason to doubt her. If he accepted that as the truth, then the only question remaining was what he was going to do about it. Unfortunately murder was out, and he couldn't just pack up and leave as he'd always done before when he'd found himself in a sticky situation. Like it or not, since his entire life savings were tied up in this place, he had no choice but to stay put and tough it out.

"No! That shifty old schemer is not going to get away with this!" he finally burst out in frustration, shattering the tense silence.

"Absolutely not!" Terry declared stoutly. "Nobody, not even my grandfather, has the right to arrange my life for me. If and when I ever decide to get remarried, it will be to a man that I've handpicked myself, and I intend to tell him that first thing in the morning!"

"And I'll be right behind you," Jess promised darkly.

The silence that followed that declaration was almost comforting. Terry was pleased to find out that, in this instance at least, she and Jess were staunch allies, and he was equally delighted by the tone in which she'd just voiced her opinion. First thing tomorrow morning, vengeance would be theirs, he concluded in satisfaction, until he realized that their self-righteous anger was not a solution to their basic problem.

"But what happens after that?" Jess demanded, dropping his feet off the coffee table as he turned to glare at her. "No matter how we feel about it, our partnership is still legal and binding."

Terry had already arrived at the same conclusion, but unlike Jess, she didn't appear to be upset. "And no matter how Grandpa Sam feels about it, that's exactly how we're going to proceed from now on, like business partners. We may have to share this house, but we'll keep everything else on a strictly impersonal basis," she informed him smoothly, then thrust out her hand. "Agreed?"

Jess stared down at her hand for several seconds, not sure he was capable of operating under those kinds of restrictions with her even if he wanted to, but then he thought about Sam's reaction to her proposal, and he smiled. Like him, Terry wanted to get some of her own back, prove to her grandfather that his scheme had backfired, and Jess was more than willing to help her settle that score. As far as the score that still needed to be settled between themselves, that would just have to be accomplished behind the scenes.

"Agreed," he stated firmly. "From now on, as far as Sam's concerned, you and I are a united front."

Seven

Feeling as if the weight of the world had just been lifted off her shoulders, Terry announced. "I'm starving. How about you?"

"I could eat," Jess admitted, and found himself alone on the couch the moment the words were out of his mouth.

Not in as big a hurry to get to the kitchen, Jess picked up the tray off the coffee table, then ambled after her. Terry was reaching inside the open refrigerator and pulling out a platter of leftover chicken when he entered the room. "Do you want me to carve some meat off the bone and make you a sandwich, or would you rather eat it like this?" she inquired, as she placed the platter and a loaf of pumpernickel down on the table, then picked up a chicken leg and bit into it.

"Is there another leg?" Jess asked politely, his eyes going very wide as she returned from the refrigerator with her arms full of jars and plastic containers. Apparently, when she said starving, she really meant starving. "Uh...maybe I should get us a couple of plates and some silverware?"

With her teeth clamped around a chicken bone, Terry didn't respond to that suggestion, but noting the ravenous expression on her face as she began tearing off lids, Jess realized that if he wanted to be included in this impromptu feast, he'd better forego his manners. By the time he'd set the tray down on the counter, crossed over to the table, and pulled out a chair for himself, Terry had finished the piece of chicken and was hungrily eyeing the deviled eggs. Since there were only two of those left on the plate, Jess reached out in front of her, grabbed an egg, and popped it into his mouth.

From the opposite side of the table, glittering brown eyes dared him to try and grab the remaining one, but as Jess took Terry up on that challenge, he discovered that her hand was far quicker then her eye. With a smug little grin, she stuffed the last egg into her mouth. Next she reached across the table for the last fluffy buttermilk biscuit.

During the past few weeks, Jess had developed more than a passing fondness for her homemade biscuits, and considering the amount of them he consumed at every meal, Terry had to know it. "Unfair," he complained. "I had my eye on that biscuit first! Now give it back."

Terry gave him a cheeky grin before biting into the soft dough. "Too late," she mumbled unrepentantly. "I'm already eating it."

"You want a fight, lady? You got it," Jess warned, his eyes gleaming with malicious intent as he grabbed for the bowl of cherry gelatin she was safeguarding in the crook of her arm. But Terry didn't relinquish her hold, and when he tugged on the edge of the container it tipped and spilled the jiggling red dessert all over the floor.

Terry started to laugh uncontrollably and Jess soon joined in. Finally, between bursts of giggles, she said, "Looks like you win."

Jess pitched in to help her clean up the mess they'd made, and she smiled conspiratorially at him and he smiled back, both of them slightly astonished at the unexpected new facet their outrageous behavior had just brought to their relationship.

Jess, in particular, was having a difficult time trying to decipher his feelings. Behaving like an irresponsible kid again had been fun, a devil-may-care good time that had been made even more enjoyable by the ridiculous efforts of his cohort in crime. Knowing that a mature, sophisticated woman like Terry was capable of practically having a food fight forced him to reevaluate his entire concept of her. Suddenly it wasn't just her beautiful body that he yearned to play with, and that realization stunned him.

"Thank goodness the boys are asleep," Terry said, as Jess carried an empty plate over to the sink and she wiped a long red smear off the oilcloth. "If they'd seen us in action tonight, we'd be scraping gelatin off the walls for the next year."

Jess nodded sheepishly, even after admitting to himself that he hadn't enjoyed himself so much in years. Something else he hadn't done for a very long time was look back on those days when having fun had been his top priority. "My three brothers and I got into a lot of trouble one time for messing up the kitchen, and we did far more damage than this," he recalled with a chuckle. "We started out by using our spoons to catapult our peas, but then we really got carried away and tried hitting each other with our mashed potatoes. My Aunt Ophelia was none too happy with us that day."

Terry paused in her wiping, aware that this was the first time Jess had ever volunteered a personal tidbit about himself. Considering his reputation as a loner, it surprised her to hear that he had three brothers as well as an extended family. For a few seconds she didn't dare ask more questions about his background for fear that he'd close up on her like a clam, but he seemed so amused by his childhood memory that she decided to take the risk. "You weren't even in your own house? You and your brothers got into a food fight at the home of a relative?"

Jess was standing over by the stove, warming up the coffee left over in the pot. "No, it was our house," he replied as he refilled their mugs and carried them back to the table. "After our folks died of influenza, we were taken in by our three great-aunts, Carrie, Winnie, and Ophelia, but Ophelia was the one we boys really had to look out for. She was the oldest sister, already in her early fifties when we five young'ns arrived on her doorstep, but let me tell ya, she could still wield a mightily mean willow switch.''

Jess wasn't aware of the accent that crept into his voice as he talked about his relatives, but Terry noticed it and also his somewhat folksy turn of phrase. ''In what part of the country was this?''

''West Virginia,'' Jess came back easily. ''We lived on the outskirts of a little podunk town called Hillsboro, population one thousand and two.''

''That's a long way from Montana,'' Terry observed as she sat down in the chair opposite him and took a sip of coffee from the mug he'd set down in front of her place. ''But that population sounds familiar. I think Milton, which is the closest town around here, can boast about the same number of people.''

Jess smiled. ''What do you know about that? Looks like you and I have something else in common besides a talent for abusing perfectly good food.''

''If we keep working at it, maybe we can come up with a few more things,'' Terry suggested, curiosity prompting her to inquire. ''Is your family still living back there?''

Jess nodded as he took a sip of coffee. ''My aunts are in their seventies now, but they're still going strong. All three of my brothers work for the local paper mill, and my younger sister, Gloria, is married to the owner of the company.''

An indulgent smile tugged up the corners of his mouth as he thought about his baby sister. Usually his thoughts about Glory were centered on those days when she'd made a real pest of herself by always following him around. Of course, she wasn't that impish little girl anymore, but some things never changed. She could still be a pest. "Glory's the one who makes sure I'm always filled in on what's happening with the family. I've never been great at writing letters, but if I let too much time go by without contacting them, Glory calls me up to give me hell. The last time I talked to her, she'd just delivered twin girls."

"So you're an uncle?"

"Six times over," Jess replied, grinning at Terry's incredulous expression. "Zeke and David are still bachelors, but my oldest brother, Ken, has two boys and two girls."

"I thought you said you didn't know that much about kids," she accused without any heat.

"I don't," Jess insisted. "I left town a couple of years before Ken got married, and I've only been back a few times since."

"Why?"

Jess seemed taken aback by the question. "Why what?"

"Why haven't you gone back to visit them more often?" Terry inquired. "Don't you ever get lonely and start missing them?"

After a long pause, during which he appeared to be contemplating a totally foreign concept, he admitted, "I left home at eighteen, and I'll admit I was real homesick that first year, but since then...well...I suppose I've just been too busy to think much about it."

"Busy doing what?"

Jess shrugged, reluctant to admit that while in pursuit of his goal, he'd put practically every other aspect of his life on hold, especially his attachment to family. He'd left home with the intention of making his own way in the world, establishing a place for himself, and that's exactly what he'd done. To some people, he supposed, that single-minded effort might be viewed as an obsession, and he didn't much like the possibility that those people could be right.

Unconsciously he fingered his lucky gold piece, remembering the advice his Aunt Ophelia had given him on the night she'd presented it to him. "Use this for luck unless you get in real desperate straits." Even though he'd been in desperate straits several times during those first few years out on his own, not once had he considered spending the coin.

Whenever he'd felt as if things couldn't get worse, he'd remembered the legacy passed down to him from his Great-Great-Grandmother Cornelia Hubbard, a story that always made him try to look on the bright side. At the close of the Civil War, that courageous lady had been alone on the farm with five small children and no menfolk to protect her, but somehow she'd managed to persevere through several long years of hardship. Even when attacked by a bushwhacker, Cornelia hadn't allowed her spirit to be broken. She'd shot the man who'd stolen her honor, and as a repayment for his crime against her, she'd kept the sack of gold coins he'd stolen from the Union Army. A God-fearing woman, she hadn't used what she'd considered "blood money" on mere frivolities. Her children had been on the brink of starvation before she'd spent her first coin.

The Hubbard family had kept Cornelia's secret for over a hundred years, each generation abiding by the terms she'd set down for using those ill-gotten gains. According to the story, good luck followed those who used the coins wisely, and those who did not were said to experience untold suffering. Of course, no one could recall anyone who'd foolishly frittered his money away, but that didn't change the family's perception of the story.

Unlike his superstitious Great-Aunt Ophelia, Jess hadn't placed much credence in Cornelia's dire warnings, but he still hadn't spent the coin. That twenty-dollar gold piece was visual proof of his connection to a long line of strong, proud, hardworking people, a tangible reminder of his tie to a loyal, loving family. Whenever he looked at it, he could picture Aunt Ophelia's careworn face, hear the deep affection in her voice, and he was reminded that no matter what the distance between himself and the rest of his kin, he would forever hold a place in their hearts.

Somewhere along the line, however, he'd allowed those family ties to loosen. Except for the monthly checks he sent to his aunts, the duty phone calls he made to the family on important holidays, he'd all but severed the connection.

In recent days, being around another man's sons and their beautiful mother, the thought had occurred to him that owning a piece of land and doing the kind of work he loved, just might not be enough to keep him satisfied for the rest of his days. Tonight, after sharing a totally nonsensical exchange with Terry, he'd been struck by that notion again, and he found it extremely disturbing. The day he'd signed the paper that declared him a half owner of the Triple L he thought he'd finally attained all that he'd ever wanted for himself, but now, he was no longer that certain.

Maybe he needed more . . . much, much more.

If, indeed, that turned out to be the case, then he'd also be forced to accept that he'd been operating under a set of totally misguided priorities for the past fifteen years. Until Terry had posed that pointed question to him, he'd never thought much about being lonely, and he certainly hadn't spent much time dwelling on the possibility that he'd given the people he cared most about every reason to think that he didn't care about them at all.

"You've been too busy doing what to think much about your family?" Terry persisted impatiently, but it wasn't her irritated tone that made Jess glower. It was the realization that over the years, he'd become an arrogant, unfeeling, self-centered son of a—

"Busy doing what?" Terry insisted more loudly.

"Working!" he snapped, irrationally angry with her for refusing to let go of a subject that painfully reinforced his newfound opinion of himself. "Busting my butt to make enough money so I could buy into this ranch."

Ignoring his forbidding tone, Terry began the line of questioning she'd been dying to put to him for weeks. "Speaking of which, just how does an itinerant cowboy who rarely gets more than a passing wage save up that kind of money by the time he's thirty?"

"I'm almost thirty-five," Jess reminded her, then smirked in the hopes of diverting their conversation in a different direction. "Are you suggesting that I don't act my age?"

Terry refused to be sidetracked from the original subject. "From the sounds of it, you left home with nothing but the shirt on your back, and according to Grandpa, you spent the last five years as a foreman for some big cattle spread in Colorado. True?"

Jess sighed in resignation. "True."

"So how in heck were you able to plunk down enough cash to pay off Sam's loans with the bank, plus all the back taxes he owed? I happen to know what a ranch foreman makes, and you couldn't have saved that much money in five years, even if you were employed by the largest spread in the country. What did you do before the Colorado job, rob banks?"

Highly insulted, Jess raised an arrogant brow at her. "I thought Sam convinced you that all those nasty suspicions you were harboring against me were absolutely groundless?"

"Grandpa convinced me that you know your way around a cattle ranch, and that he trusts your decisions concerning the Triple L, but what does that prove?" Terry demanded tartly. "Sam's also been known to place his trust in snake oil salesmen, traveling rain dancers, and used car dealers."

"Good point," Jess acknowledged dryly, then groused with annoyance, "But that still doesn't make me a bank robber or even a con man. I'll have you know I've come by every cent I've ever made by honest means."

That claim didn't appease Terry's curiosity in the slightest, and she just sat there in expectant silence, waiting for him to continue. Jess glared at her, but her expression didn't alter until he burst out in exasperation, "Okay, you nosy little busybody! I struck it rich in the Oklahoma oil fields!"

"Come now. Surely, you don't expect me to believe that you're some kind of oil baron," Terry exclaimed incredulously, focusing a pointed gaze on his holey T-shirt and faded gray sweats.

Jess cocked his head to one side. "I guess you'd have to say I'm more like a minibaron, since I only own a ten percent share in one well, but..." He held up his hand to prevent Terry from making any sarcastic remarks. "When that well came in it was a real gusher. Of course, it went dry a few years back, but by that time, I'd accumulated a very sizable nest egg."

"So you worked for a time as a wildcatter," Terry said, and since she found that so easy to believe, she made no attempt to pose the statement as a question. From the first Jess had struck her as the adventurous type, a man who loved to take risks, and he had just confirmed it. Unfortunately it was that evaluation of his character that made it impossible for her to trust in his ability to settle down anywhere on a permanent basis. One of these days he was going to lose interest in the challenge presented by the Triple L and he would move on to some other venture.

Unaware that he was only adding more credence to that belief, Jess told her about some of the other jobs he'd held down over the past fifteen years. "I started out working as a lumberjack in the southern pine forests of Georgia, but then I got itchy feet and signed up with a road crew that was heading farther west. When I got tired of working that job, I took a training course and drove a ten-wheeler out of Little Rock, Arkansas. I did that for about nine months or so before I met Charley Oaks. He's the guy who convinced me that there were opportunities to be made as a wildcatter, and believe it or not, our very first well came in.''

''I'm more than willing to believe that you're incredibly lucky,'' Terry grumbled, repeating the accusation she'd made to him on the day they first met. ''You were certainly in the right spot at the right time when it came to buying this ranch.''

''Now that I know what I was actually letting myself in for,'' Jess said, annoyed by her sour tone, ''I'd be hard put to classify that as an amazing stroke of good luck.''

Terry lifted her chin at a haughty angle, her dark eyes shooting sparks. ''If that's the way you feel, I'd be happy to help you change your ill fortune. My offer to buy you out still holds.''

The last thing Jess wanted was to get into another argument with her, but after that provoking comment, he had no choice but to retaliate. ''Great,'' he declared scathingly, knowing exactly how much money she'd been able to invest. ''Give me five hundred thousand in cash, and the Triple L is all yours.''

''Five hundred thousand!''

''In cash.''

"But that's outrageous," Terry sputtered. "Even if I did have that kind of money, which I don't, this place isn't worth nearly that much!"

"Well, that shows exactly how much you know about it," Jess informed her. "The land itself is worth more than that."

Terry was much too astonished to react to the blow he'd just dealt to her pride. "It is!" she exclaimed. "You're positively sure about that?"

"I'm sure."

"But the profits from our cattle operation don't come anywhere close to that number," she observed, much more cognizant of the meaning behind the phrase Land Rich, But Cash Poor that was often used in reference to farmers.

"They'll come a lot closer once I'm through," Jess assured her arrogantly.

"I hope so," Terry surprised him by saying, then annoyed him again with her next comment. "At least you're not starting out that far in the hole. It may have taken a great deal of money to pay off Sam's loans, but if you'd had to repurchase half the land to become an owner, even a rich minioil baron like you couldn't have afforded it."

"No, I couldn't," Jess admitted. "But Sam didn't make such a bad deal for himself. The ranch is debt free, up to date on its taxes, and I've got the know-how to make it into one of the most profitable operations in three states. I'll admit that's going to take some time, but believe me, it will happen."

"I'd be much more willing to believe you if you also had a reputation for staying in one spot for more than a couple of years at a time."

"I'm not going anywhere," Jess countered tersely, and as far as he was concerned, that put an end to the discussion. He stood up from the table. "Now that we've got all that settled, I think I'll go up to bed. It's getting late."

"Leave this room, buster, and you'll be very sorry!"

Jess's mouth dropped open and his eyes widened as she jumped up from her chair and faced him. "You're threatening me, Terry?" he inquired slowly, just to make sure he hadn't misunderstood.

"You bet I am."

"And you think you've got the means to back up that threat?"

Grasping the edge of the table with both hands, Terry leaned forward, her chin thrust out at a belligerent angle as she declared, "If you ever want to sink your teeth into another batch of my buttermilk biscuits, Jess Hubbard, you'd be wise to sit yourself right back down."

Once her words got through to him, Jess found it extremely hard to maintain his fierce expression, but somehow he managed. He stood there for several seconds, glaring back at her, but even though her brown eyes were twinkling merrily, she didn't crack a smile. "You fight real dirty, lady," he accused before grasping the back of his chair and swiveling the seat around so he could straddle it. "Okay, so I'm sitting. Now what?"

"Now, we're going to discuss the prejudicial division of power around here, and how it's going to be changed," Terry stated firmly, keeping a close eye on him as she slowly lowered herself back down into a seated position. "Thus far, I've been relegated to the position of chief cook and bottle washer, but if you and Sam want to continue enjoying your meals, you'll give me a much bigger say in the business end of things."

"In other words," Jess said, "this is blackmail."

Terry didn't look the least bit horrified by that summation. Indeed, she appeared to be remarkably pleased by her own cunning. "Wonderful cook that I am, I can easily spoil the broth . . . or not. The choice is up to you."

Lips twitching, Jess growled in mock frustration, "I repeat, lady. You fight real dirty."

Terry smiled with supreme feminine satisfaction. "A woman has to do what a woman has to do."

"And what exactly is that?" Jess inquired.

Terry explained her position, starting with her desire to be included on all future management decisions and ending with an offer to take over all the bookkeeping, a job that she noticed both Jess and Sam studiously avoided. Since Jess didn't even balk at that suggestion, she announced, "I also have some ideas about the future use of our present cash reserves. Rebuilding the quality of our stock, improving our range land, and constructing a more efficient handling system for our herd are all necessary, but this place is also a home for people, not just animals."

When Jess merely looked at her, his expression re-
vealing nothing, Terry continued, "Apparently, you
and Sam haven't noticed, but this house is practically
falling down around our heads. The plumbing and
fixtures in the bathroom are extremely outdated, that
old furnace might not make it through another winter, and the kitchen is an antiquated joke. I think we
should consider using part of our reserve account for
some immediate remodeling."

Jess remained silent for a long time, but Terry was
unaware of the turbulent inner struggle he was fighting. Before she'd bought a quarter share of the ranch,
there hadn't been any cash reserves, and the account
she kept referring to was comprised entirely of her own
money. A part of him wanted to tell her that she could
spend her cash in any way she saw fit, that he had no
intention of touching it, but another part recognized
that an influx of ready cash would speed up the process of turning the Triple L around. If he could go out
and purchase the breeders he required, instead of
waiting until his best yearlings matured and started
reproducing, he could increase the quality of the herd
in far less time than he'd originally planned.

Being cash poor was a perpetual problem for a large
majority of ranchers, but if he could somehow manage to swallow his pride, it wouldn't have to be his
biggest problem. Terry considered the money she'd
invested as their money, not just hers. Unfortunately
Jess had trouble seeing things her way. Even if he did
accept the concept, and that was a very big if, he certainly wouldn't spend a single dime on remodeling the
house.

On the other hand, he could see why Terry would find that idea so appealing. Having a nice house was extremely important to a woman. Women were nesters, and even he had to admit that this nest wasn't in the best of shape. For two single men, like him and Sam, the house was more than adequate, but Terry was used to far better. If nothing else, her ex-husband had provided her with a large, well-furnished home, something Jess wouldn't be able to provide for her or any other women for at least a couple more years. Even if everything went his way, the best he could hope for this year was to break even.

"You think that's a really dumb idea, don't you?" Terry asked, unable to stand the silence any longer. "Even if we're forced to huddle next to the fireplace all winter long in order to stay warm, you still think the needs of the herd should come first."

Jess took a deep breath, still not certain which side of the fence he wanted to be on. "I think you should decide how you want to spend the money you've invested, but if you asked my opinion, yes. I'd use most of it to buy the highest quality stock I could afford and the rest on an automated feeding system and the building materials for a new cattle barn."

Terry was more than willing to compromise. "How about if we spend half of the money to buy stock, a quarter of it to secure a loan for a new barn and feeding system, and the last quarter to update the house?"

"We just got this place out of debt and I don't want to start that ball rolling again."

"Okay, I can understand that," Terry agreed. "But I do have to think about the boys, Jess, and children require a home with adequate heat. A new furnace is an absolute necessity.''

Yes, Jess thought, she did have to think about her boys, and he had to think about disease, bad weather, poor crops, and lousy prices. ''Fine,'' he stated softly. ''We'll get a new furnace.''

Terry smiled at him. ''And we'll also think about redoing that awful bathroom?''

''Sure,'' Jess said, faking a yawn. ''Now, is that it, Terry? It's been one hell of a long day, and I'm tired.''

''That's it,'' Terry replied, and stood up, but Jess didn't wait for her to precede him out of the room. He made what she thought was an extremely abrupt departure. When she got to the bottom of the stairs, he was already striding down the second floor hall as if anxious to put as much distance between them as possible.

''Good night,'' she murmured, a few seconds later, as she passed by his bedroom, but there was no response from the other side of the closed door. ''I know I was pushing my luck when I brought up the bathroom,'' she chastised herself, but even if she had to put up with another year of tepid showers, she was more than satisfied with everything else she'd managed to accomplish tonight. At long last, she and Jess were really starting to communicate.

Eight

The following day, after a fruitless confrontation with Sam the matchmaker, who accused them of having suspicious minds, Jess and Terry established a routine that seemed to work well for both of them. For the next week Terry kept herself busy with the chores that needed to be done near the homestead, and Jess stayed as far from the vicinity as possible, knowing that was the only way he could manage to keep his hands off her.

Unfortunately at this time of the year, once all the fences were mended, there wasn't that much else left to do out on the range, so Jess was grateful when the crew of hired hands arrived to help with the roundup. Except for mealtimes, he was too busy overseeing the branding to notice Terry. Of course, as per their new policy, he knew where she could be found most evenings. Immediately after supper, she closed herself inside the study to do the ranch's paperwork. Jess studiously avoided that room.

After listening to Terry outline her ideas concerning their partnership, Jess was determined that he wouldn't be the first one to admit that their "strictly business" arrangement didn't stand one chance in hell of working. He didn't realize that his eyes automatically strayed toward the study door every night when he returned to the house, but Sam noticed and he took great delight in pointing it out.

"Looks to me like that old adage just ain't working, now is it, Jess?"

Having spent a long, hard day in the saddle, every muscle in his body ached, and all Jess wanted to do when he'd joined Sam in the living room was stretch out on the soft cushions of the couch, close his eyes, and relax. He'd been glad to find that the boys had already gone up to bed, for he certainly didn't feel much like playing video games or talking, but of course that didn't stop Sam from starting up a conversation the instant he'd made himself comfortable. "What old adage?" he inquired, hoping his irritable tone would give Sam the message.

"The one that says Out Of Sight, Out Of Mind."

Jess lifted the arm he'd placed over his eyes and grudgingly turned his head toward Sam's chair, scowling when the older man lowered his newspaper to reveal a smug smile. "What the hell are you talking about?"

"You can deny it till the cows come home," Sam replied loftily. "But the first thing you do when you walk through that door every night is look for Terry, which tells me she's always on your mind.''

Jess was too startled by that observation to comment, but a few seconds later, he growled, ''You're imagining things, old man.'' Unfortunately his telltale pause was all the confirmation that Sam needed.

''It doesn't take much of an imagination to know what's going on in your head, or that many brains to figure out that you're running scared,'' he retorted sarcastically. ''And I told that same thing to Terry.''

Jess's reaction to that remark was instantaneous. He sat up like a shot, nostrils flaring as he demanded, ''You told what to Terry?''

''That making calf's eyes at you when she thinks you're not looking is just plain cowardly,'' Sam replied. ''Even if I *am* responsible for putting a few wheels into motion, and I ain't saying I am, that's no reason for you two to stamp so blasted hard on the brakes.''

Jess completely ignored the last part of Sam's self-righteous speech, but he couldn't ignore his first comment. ''You've seen Terry making calf's eyes at me!''

''She spends half her time spying on you through the kitchen curtains.''

Jess slumped back on the couch, trying to digest that intriguing bit of information, thoroughly delighted by the news. Then he remembered who had delivered it and he pulled himself up short. ''Once you glom on to an idea, old man, you simply refuse to give up on it, don't you? Well, I'm sorry, but this time, I'm not falling for it.''

Sam rolled his eyes, then snorted in disgust, tossed his paper down on the floor, and stood up from his chair. "Hell! You've fallen so hard, Jess Hubbard, that you can't even think straight!"

The truth hurt some people, but it made others extremely angry. "I have not fallen for Terry!"

Sam nodded. "Right. You keep telling yourself that, boy," he suggested dryly. "You still won't convince me, but one of these days, you just might be able to convince yourself."

For the rest of that night and the entire next day Jess struggled to do just that. He struggled long and hard, punishing anyone or anything that tried to break his concentration. He snapped at the hired hands, snarled at the cattle, and swore at his horse, but by sundown, he'd succeeded in his quest. He felt a great many things for Terry, but he didn't love her. He liked her spunky personality, admired her determined spirit, respected her volatile temper, and appreciated her beauty. And above and beyond everything else, he lusted after her body. Sam was right, for *that* reason, she *was* constantly on his mind.

Jess's mood lightened considerably upon reaching that conclusion. Lust was a feeling he could deal with. Over the years, he'd become very familiar with the needs of his body and how to satisfy them. Unlike love, lust was something a man could control and do something about. Love was a fatal emotion, but lust was easily remedied.

Naturally a woman like Terry wouldn't appreciate his less than honorable intentions toward her, but she was a practical person, and eventually she'd have to accept the inevitable, just as he'd accepted it. With any luck, he could persuade her to accept it before he went totally out of his mind.

Feeling much more in command of himself, Jess stayed outside in the horse barn for another half hour that night, making up to Dusty for mistreating him earlier in the day. He gave the stallion a brisk rub-down, then got out the curry brush and went to work, brushing away every speck of dust that had accumu-lated on the animal's broad back. "Next week that pretty filly I purchased over in Bozeman is scheduled to arrive, and then you'll understand what I've been going through lately," he declared apologetically. "And I'm warning you now, son, surrender to those feelings early, or you'll really be hurting, just like I am."

The stallion snorted, and Jess laughed. "Doubt me if you want, but romancing a woman is hell, Dus-ty...pure, unadulterated hell. No self-respecting male should have to endure this kind of torture. I've had just about enough of it, and believe me, fella, first chance I get, I intend to do something about that."

"Do something about what?" Terry asked, as she stepped up on the lowest rail and folded her arms over the top of the stall.

Jess turned his head at the sound of her voice, his eyes smoldering in response to her question, reflect-ing the heat that her presence instantly inspired much lower down in his body. She had dressed for the oc-casion, he noted wolfishly, glancing between the rails of the stall to admire the tight fit of her jeans and the bright red tube top that left her shoulders bare and showed off the delectable curves of her breasts. As always, looking at her made him feel a bit crazy, but tonight he vowed, he was taking the cure.

Holding her questioning gaze, he gave Dusty a farewell pat on the muzzle, then stepped out of the stall. "I'll be happy to show you," he drawled smoothly, catching hold of her elbow as he rounded the corner. "That is, if you don't mind taking a walk with me."

"It's a beautiful night for a walk," Terry agreed breathlessly, half-running in order to keep up with him as they left the barn. "But at this pace, I'm not sure I'll be able to last very long."

"Then I'll be sure to take it real slow," he promised, smiling inwardly as he dropped her arm and decreased the length of his stride. "Then you'll be with me right up to the end."

Terry noticed the gleam of amusement in his eyes and almost sighed in relief. According to Sam, Jess had been in a hellish mood all day. One of the wranglers had already quit and several more had threatened to do so if he behaved that churlishly toward them again tomorrow. Since Sam had been yelled at a number of times himself, he'd told the other men to take their complaints up with Terry, and she'd reluctantly agreed to speak to Jess on their behalf.

Apparently he'd recovered from whatever had been bothering him earlier, but just in case there was some problem that she, as his business partner, should be made aware of, she decided not to completely forego the subject. "I understand there was some trouble during the branding today," she began calmly, stating the facts in the form of a question. "You were angry with a few of the men?"

"I was angry with all of the men," Jess corrected wryly. "But I got over it."

"Weren't they working fast enough to suit you?"

Jess shook his head. "They were doing fine, I just had a nasty burr under my hide, and it took me awhile to work it out."

"I see," Terry replied evenly, thinking he might be more specific if she gave him the right opening. "Of course, it wouldn't surprise me if everybody was feeling a tad irritable today. It must have reached ninety degrees this afternoon."

"We were all sweating out there," Jess concurred, but his tone implied that the heat hadn't been the prime motivation for his bad temper, and Terry gave up trying to get to the root of the problem.

"Did Sam tell you that Larry Able quit?"

"That's no big loss," Jess declared with an uncaring shrug. "But I suppose I'd better apologize to the other men just in case they're tempted to do the same."

"I think that might be a good idea," Terry conceded, relieved that her task had been accomplished so easily. "Where are we walking? It's almost dark outside so we should probably avoid the woods."

Jess paid no heed to her warning but kept on in the direction of the creek. "You're not afraid of tripping over a dead log or falling over a tree stump?" she asked.

"We won't do that if we stick to the path," Jess replied. "When we reach the end of it, we can follow the creek bed until it cuts around near the south pasture." He pointed toward the rapidly darkening sky, where a few twinkling stars could already be seen. "On a clear night like this, the moon will light our way back across the field."

Jess was describing a route Terry had taken so many times as a child that she probably had every step of the way memorized. Although the last of the sun disappeared before they'd gone even halfway, neither one of them stumbled as they walked along the narrow path, but Terry couldn't help but feel a tiny shiver of apprehension as they approached the creek. The last time she'd come this way was the day of the electrical storm, and she and Jess had ended up rolling around half-naked on the damp, stone floor of a cave.

She had to wonder if Jess wasn't thinking about the same incident when they reached her "thinking rock" and he came to an abrupt halt, but when she glanced over at him, he was gazing in the opposite direction, staring down into the moonlit water of the creek. "What are you looking for?" she inquired, noting that he seemed to be trying to locate something beneath the shimmering depths.

He pointed to a dark section of water beneath a fallen birch tree that formed a natural bridge across the width of the creek. "How deep would you say it is under there?"

Thinking that he was feeling adventurous and wanted to test his skill at log walking, she informed him, "I know it doesn't look that deep, but that's where the underground spring comes up and there's a big hole right under that branch. If you fall off of it, you'll go right in over your head."

"That's what I thought, but I needed confirmation," he declared in satisfaction as he dropped down on the ground and started taking off his boots.

"What are you doing!"

"I'm going in," he replied matter-of-factly, already barefoot as he looked up at her. "Aren't you coming?"

Terry thought back to what he'd said in the barn. "This was what you wanted to show me?"

Jess paused in unbuttoning his shirt, his expression slightly sheepish, "To be honest, I was hoping that you'd be the one to show me," he confessed. "You grew up here so I figured you'd know the best place to swim. It's a perfect night for skinny-dipping, don't you think?"

At the sight of his bare chest, Terry wasn't capable of much thinking, but when he reached for the belt buckle on his jeans, she managed a high-pitched protest, "You're not getting totally naked!"

"That's how most people define skinny-dipping," Jess reminded her, then proving that he possessed absolutely no sense of modesty, he stripped off his jeans and briefs. "Don't you?"

When he turned around to face her, Terry's breath caught in her throat, and her heart began to pound. She couldn't have spoken a word even if she tried. Moonlight played across his bronzed skin, highlighting his beautiful hair to a metallic sheen. As if cast in silver by a sculptor's hand, the masculine planes and angles of his body glowed in opalescent splendor against a backdrop of forest shadow. The haze of curling golden hair that covered his flesh glowed in the light, glorifying the lines and power of his magnificent structure.

"Heaven help me," Terry moaned, as she drank in the beauty of his nakedness, but luckily, Jess didn't hear her choked-sounding plea. As she stood there frozen in shock, he waded into the water, and when she finally regained control of the use of her limbs, he was gone. All she saw was a flash of golden skin above the fine white mist that rose up around the edges of the small pool, and it took her a full thirty seconds to realize that he'd dived under the surface.

As she stared at the ever widening ripples that circled the spot where he'd disappeared, she shivered, remembering how cold the spring-fed water could be. When he didn't immediately resurface, Terry began to grow frightened. What if the shock of that cold water had been too much for him? Caused a debilitating cramp?

In a matter of seconds, she had stripped down to her strapless bra and panties and she already had one foot in the water when Jess came back up for air. Unaware that she was in a state of near panic, he chuckled at her semichaste attire. "At least you're not a total priss," he teased, using the flat of his palm to shoot a light spray of water over her head before he jackknifed below the surface again.

Terry closed her eyes, waiting for the rush of adrenaline to subside so she would stop shaking. She willed herself to breathe slowly, in and out, in and out, until she'd established a near normal rhythm. Of course, an extremely furious person couldn't entirely control her rapid breathing, and not even being doused with a spray of cold water could quench the fiery heat of her temper. In fact, that uncalled-for attack on her person had only served to fan the flames.

A few seconds later she opened her eyes, placed both hands on her hips, and issued fair warning to the naked man floating so comfortably on the silvery stretch of water beneath the birch tree. "I think I may just have to kill you, Jess Hubbard!"

Startled by the sincerity in her tone, Jess let his legs drop below the surface, then began treading water as he watched her determined stride through the shallow portion of the stream. "What did I do?" he demanded, brows lifting when she reached the semicircular drop-off at the edge of the deep pool, shot him a murderous look, then lifted her arms and dived in.

Fortunately since his mouth was already open, Jess was able to swallow a gulp of air before he was dragged underwater. When Terry released him from her grip around his legs, he shot up to the surface.

"Jeezus!" he sputtered. "You half drowned me!"

Terry pushed her wet hair off her face, and her serene expression made Jess even madder. He was tempted to give her a dose of her own medicine, but she swam out of reach before he could grab her, then lifted one of her arms and waggled a finger at him. "It serves you right for scaring me like that," she informed him tartly.

"Scare you?" Jess demanded, grabbing hold of a low overhanging branch from the birch tree to keep himself afloat. "What did I do to scare you?"

"You stayed underwater so long I was sure you'd been crippled by a cramp," she exclaimed indignantly. "And then...and then, you despicable man, you had the utter gall to splash cold water all over me when I was coming to your rescue."

Jess looked at her incredulously. An instant later he was smiling, happy to think that she'd rush to his aid even if there hadn't been the slightest need. "I'm sorry, Terry," he apologized, in a low, soothing tone. "I never meant to scare you like that. I guess I should've warned you that I can swim like a fish and hold my breath for one hel...heck of a long time."

Having expended most of her excess energy on her fierce underwater assault, Terry was willing to be appeased, and she returned Jess's penitent smile as she grabbed hold of a branch and pulled herself through the water until she found a firm footing. No longer fearing his retaliation, she bobbed next to him in the water, but then she relaxed even more and allowed her legs to float out in front of her body. With a soft sigh, she rested her head back against the gentle ripples of the pond and gazed up at the starry summer sky, amazed with herself for feeling so content. "I have to admit, after such a hot day, this really does feel wonderful."

Jess turned his body until it was parallel to hers, then matched her horizontal position. "Mmm," he murmured in agreement, hoping the languid motion of the cool water would wash away each and every one of her inhibitions. In the meantime he would simply lie back and enjoy the view, but his heated gaze wasn't directed toward the stars. It was on the beautiful woman floating next to him in the water, seemingly unconcerned that when wet, her white lace panties and matching bra had turned completely transparent. As far as he was concerned, that was an excellent start.

"I used to come swimming here almost every day in the summer when I was a girl," Terry said. "I imagine the boys will want to do the same once they discover it, which they will, since they set off exploring every chance they get."

A few weeks ago Jess couldn't imagine himself asking this kind of question, but so much had changed since then that it came out automatically. "They both know how to swim, don't they?"

"Like little eels," Terry assured him. "Doug and I belonged to the country club, and it had an Olympic size pool that was heated all year long. I had both boys enrolled in Water Babies by the time they were six months old. Chuckie's still not too sure he likes the water that much, but Chad was on the peewee diving team two years ago, and he won a first place medal at one of the local swim meets. Of course, once my marriage was over, I lost my membership at the club, and Doug couldn't be bothered to take the boys to their swimming lessons, which was a shame, because the instructor at the club was a former Olympian."

Considering their humble, natural surroundings, Jess couldn't help but wonder if Terry regretted other losses besides the opportunity to provide her sons with a heated pool and a world-class swimming instructor. During her marriage to a wealthy, corporate lawyer, she'd lived a life of luxury in an exclusive suburb, and Jess realized that it must have been very hard for her to give up her yuppy life-style, a loss made even harder by the knowledge that her ex-husband didn't care enough about his sons to make sure they weren't deprived as well.

According to Sam, Doug Brubacker had given up his weekly visitation rights shortly after the divorce, and he'd stopped sending Terry support checks around the same time. Unless she decided to take the man back to court, which Sam predicted she wouldn't do, the settlement money she'd received after the divorce was all the money she was ever going to see. For all practical purposes, every cent she had was now tied up in the ranch.

Suddenly it became very important to Jess to find out how Terry really felt about being sentenced to spend the rest of her days on a lowly cattle ranch in the middle of nowhere. "The boys don't act as if they miss Chicago, but at their ages, kids are pretty happy anywhere. How about you, Terry? Do you miss life in the city?"

"I thought I would," Terry admitted honestly. "But I don't. In fact, I realized that I never was going to miss it on my drive here from Butte. The closer I got to the Triple L, the better I felt, and since then I've discovered that my heart never really left this place even though I made the mistake of leaving here."

"You were in love," Jess reminded her, even though he experienced an intense attack of jealousy when he imagined her making calf's eyes at some other man, a man that didn't deserve to walk on the same ground with her.

"No, I was in love with love," Terry corrected him in a tone that contained only a slight note of bitterness. "Unfortunately I chose to get married before I found out what true love is all about, and then it was too late. I'd already taken my vows and it wasn't in me to break them."

She emitted a self-deprecating laugh. "I realize that in this day and age, with divorce being so prevalent, that most people don't expect to keep those promises forever, but I did. If Doug hadn't done everything in his power to make a mockery of those vows, I'd probably still be married to him. I gave up on the hearts and flowers dream soon after the honeymoon, but I never gave up trying to make our marriage work."

Maybe he was ridiculously old-fashioned himself, but Jess couldn't laugh at her naive dreams, or fault her for respecting the solemn promises she'd made during her marriage ceremony, even though the man she'd made them to hadn't respected them in return. In truth, upon hearing her traditional beliefs, Jess felt closer to Terry than he'd ever been to any woman, including his first. He realized then that he could no longer even dredge up a clear picture of Lottie's face, which demonstrated the truth in the opinion his Great-Aunt Ophelia had always maintained.

Lottie Jean Hollister hadn't been the right woman for him. The right woman for him was a beautiful, doe-eyed brunette who could blister the hide off a man with her tongue and ride circles around him on a horse. Even if he never managed to accept her hearts and flowers definition of true love, Jess could assure Terry of one thing—if he made a promise to her, he would never break it. Unlike her ex-husband, he was a man of his word.

"Terry?"

"Mmm?"

"I really did bring you out here to show you something."

Terry should have recognized the sensual note in his husky tone, but the lack of anything sexual in their encounter had provided her with a false sense of security, and the tranquil motion of the water had lulled both her body and her brain into a state of total relaxation. "What?" she murmured drowsily.

Jess let go of the branch that had made it so easy for him to float in place, and the instant his feet were planted on the bottom of the creek bed, he reached for her. "This," he growled softly, then covered her moist, cool lips with his hot, searching mouth.

Jess felt the tiny ripple of shock that went through her as their wet, naked bodies made searing contact, but he was almost positive that her soft moan was of pleasure, not protest. To make certain of it, he lifted his mouth away from hers. Her reaction was immediate. Sliding her fingers through his hair, she pulled his head back down to her lips, and Jess needed no further proof that she wanted him just as much as he wanted her.

Terry might have attempted to deny it if Jess hadn't captured her so completely unawares, but the moment he'd kissed her, it was too late for that. Instead of drawing away, her body had instinctively moved closer, her languid limbs intertwining with his. In seconds he'd stripped her of her bra and panties, but

Terry didn't mind. She was already aching for the feel of his naked flesh against hers. When Jess cupped her bottom in his large hands, she arched her back and Jess lifted her higher against him, moving his hands around to her waist as he lowered his head to her breasts.

She groaned when his mouth closed over one nipple, his tongue encircling the sensitive tip as his lips laved the tender flesh surrounding it with liquid heat. Its twin was soon treated to identical torment and Terry arched herself higher, locking her legs around his hips. No longer worried that she might sink in the water, Jess slid his hands up the sides of her rib cage, then beneath her breasts, using his thumbs to stroke awake the tiny droplets of moisture that glistened like moonlit diamonds on her smooth, pale skin.

"Lord, Terry, I want you so much," he murmured hoarsely, and when she responded by whispering the same thing back to him, Jess drew her with him to the edge of the pool, then lifted her up in his arms and carried her out of the water.

As the shock of the cool night air hit her body, Terry experienced a brief attack of reservations, not quite certain how she'd allowed herself to get so carried away, but then Jess was laying her down on a bed of soft grasses, and when he started kissing her, she was swiftly carried away once again. She could feel the heated hardness of him surging against her, and she knew that she wanted him to possess her more than she'd ever wanted anything.

"Love me, Jess," she pleaded desperately. "Love me."

Nine

"I will," Jess assured between lips that roved over her face, then returned to her mouth to savor her exquisite taste. "I am."

As his tongue plunged into her mouth, Terry responded hungrily, wanting more, desperate for more. Nothing else seemed to matter as blind, primitive passion flared to consume them both. Desires that could no longer be controlled or channeled, only satisfied. Her fingers sought the silken smoothness of his slick wet hair, as a hungry, whimpering sound came from her throat.

Lowering his mouth, Jess tasted the satin swell of her breasts, his lips taunting, teasing, until Terry dug her hands into the hard flesh of his shoulders in an effort to assert her own needs and end the torment of his mouth. Jess wouldn't allow it. His lips closed over the dusty rose tip of one moistened breast, and she moaned in frustrated delight, twisting her body to show him that she'd already suffered enough.

Instead of taking her then, as she wanted, he increased the erotic torment, his tongue going round and round the taut, oversensitive skin of her nipples. With each circular motion, Terry felt a tightening in another part of her. Deep inside, a hot ache of pleasure demanded immediate soothing.

She opened her legs, drawing him to the ache by hooking her leg over his hip and pulling him near. She sensed his smile at her breast, felt his hand slide down between their bodies to caress the most intimate part of her, but Terry was already on fire for him, and his expert stroking brought her to such a peak of wanting that she could barely stand having him touch her there. She needed him to be inside her, to fill her with his rigid manhood.

Now...she needed him now! "Please, Jess..."

Her frantic plea was more than Jess could withstand. He too was caught in the throes of an instinct too strong to resist, and her wild little cries made it impossible. In one hard, gratifying thrust he was filling her silken, eager body. She was so hot, so incredibly tight, that he groaned. His first thrust was followed immediately by another, and another, as the wonderful pressure built up inside him, driving him closer and closer to the release he craved with every particle of his being.

At the feel of him moving within her, so strong and hard and powerful, Terry gasped, her fingers clenching in the golden hair on his chest, her head thrown back, her muscles contracting. Jess surged upward, setting a wild pace, but she matched her movements to his with remarkable ease. The tension grew to unbelievable levels, and when the final release came, it was an explosion. Terry's hands grabbed his shoulders, her neck arched, and she cried out as the violent convulsions claimed her. Jess cried out, too, as he felt the world suddenly burst into a million blinding stars.

After what seemed like hours, Jess came back to himself, felt the heat of Terry's body beneath his, her pulsing heartbeat, the tender trembling of her slender arms and long legs. He was stunned by how long it had taken him to recover his breath. Never in his life had he felt such savage surrender or been so totally drained. Yet, he also felt renewed, and that thought hammered into his brain with the same force of his wild heartbeat.

He lifted his head and searched her dark eyes, sensing that her shock equaled his. "That was incredible," he murmured hoarsely.

"More than incredible," Terry whispered back, in a tone so breathless that Jess grinned. Maybe he had taken the decision out of her hands, but now he knew that he'd done the right thing, and after the wonder they'd just shared, Terry had to realize it, too. Even if he had waited to seduce her until all of her defenses were down, she'd been totally with him at the end, begging him to possess her. Her uninhibited response to his lovemaking confirmed the conclusions he'd drawn about their relationship as nothing else could've done.

"I don't know about you, but I've got all the proof I need," he drawled, unable to resist dropping a light, tender kiss on lips that were already swollen by his kisses.

"Proof of what?" Terry managed to ask, though her mind was increasingly occupied by the knowledge that her body was still joined with his, an arousing awareness that was making it extremely difficult for her to move, let alone draw a normal breath.

"Proof that we ought to get married."

Moonlight seemed to be swirling around his golden head, making her feel dizzy as Terry gaped up at him. "Married," she repeated stupidly. "Married?" When he nodded, she practically screeched, "Married!"

Jess smiled at her dumbfounded reaction, crediting the overwhelming experience they'd just enjoyed for her inability to think logically. "After this, what other choice is there?" he inquired patiently. "Unless you expect me to sneak in your bedroom window every night for the next twenty years."

Terry's eyes widened as it sank into her brain that he was actually serious. "What happened between us tonight was probably inevitable," she admitted fervently. "But one temporary lapse in good judgment is certainly no reason for you to go off half-cocked like this!"

Jess grinned at her choice of phrasing, thrusting forward with his hips in order to provide her with a graphic demonstration of her error. "Does this feel like I'm overreacting?"

Terry gasped, then blushed scarlet as her inner muscles clenched in passionate response to his slightest movement. "Stop it!"

"See?" Jess chuckled knowingly. "We're not exactly mismatched, are we?"

Terry glared mutinously up at him, resenting the power he had over her body and resenting him for using it against her this way. "Please get off of me," she demanded hotly. "I can't breathe."

Hearing the defiance in her voice, Jess realized that she wasn't operating on the same wavelength as he was. There was no way she could deny what had just happened between them, but that's what she wanted to do, and her rejection of the obvious totally infuriated him. "You want me, Terry. Well, now you've got me, so you might as well accept the fact that we're going to get married."

"I don't accept any such thing!"

"You will," Jess assured her arrogantly, and Terry saw an almost predatory gleam in his eyes before he brought up his hand to cup her breast, then lowered his head.

"No, I—" Terry groaned when his mouth closed over her nipple, and her despairing words came out harshly. "Please, Jess! People don't get married because they're good in bed together. There has to be more to a marriage than that! Please!"

Unable to ignore her frantic plea, Jess pulled away from her and sat up, frustration etched in every line of his face as he declared bluntly, "It's enough reason for me, but if you want to get practical, there's plenty of other reasons for us to get married. For one thing, your boys need a father, and I'm not only volunteering to take on the job, I can guarantee that you won't be interviewing any other candidates. I'm the head honcho on this place, Terry. The only man available to you, and that's the way it's always going to be."

Before Terry could open her mouth to dispute his chauvinistic claim, Jess astonished her by admitting, "Before you and the boys showed up I didn't realize that I wanted a wife and a family, but I do. Chad and Chuck are great kids, and being around them has shown me that I've been missing out on something pretty wonderful. Now, when I walk into the house at night, somebody's glad to see me, and that makes me feel damned good."

"But Jess—"

"No buts about it. I'm tired of being lonely... and I'm extremely sick and tired of climbing into a cold, empty bed every night, especially when I know there's a warm, passionate woman in the very next room down the hall, a woman who wants me every bit as much as I want her."

"Jess—"

Again Terry tried to interject a few comments of her own, assuming that he was now willing to listen to her point of view since he'd given up on physical persuasion in favor of discussion, but Jess was on a real roll, and he wouldn't give her the chance to say anything. "Okay! If you don't want to consider the convenience angle, that's fine, too," he declared roundly. "I've given our entire situation quite a lot of thought, and even looking at it from a purely business standpoint, it makes sense for us to get married, especially from your end."

Terry was beginning to realize that Jess had indeed given this marriage idea a lot of thought and was also prepared to expound at great length on that thinking. Unlike him, however, she wasn't cloaked by a zealous heat. She was stark naked and shivering with cold. Unfortunately when she looked around in a desperate search for her clothes, Jess assumed she wasn't listening and grabbed her by the arm.

"Dammit, Terry!" he swore, lurching up on his knees and wrenching her up on hers. "Even if I did agree to sell you my half of the ranch, you don't have enough money to buy it outright, and the banks would never give a single woman a loan that large. After the mess Sam made of things, they won't extend him any more credit either, but I'm a young, hardworking man, and I've already impressed them with the amount of money I've been able to invest without asking for their assistance. I realize that this goes against your feminist grain, but face it, there's not a single banker around that will credit you with the ability to make a go of this place by yourself, and without a line of credit, you won't last more than a couple of years. Is that the kind of future you want for your sons?"

Obviously Jess found nothing amusing about two naked people kneeling breast to breast in the cold night air to conduct an argument, but all of a sudden, their situation struck Terry as ridiculous. So incredibly hilarious that she started to laugh, but Jess's outraged shout drowned out her helpless amusement. "Damn you, woman! This isn't funny. You need me in every way there is, and I'm not going to give up until I hear you admit it.''

Terry's mouth clamped shut as she stared into his brilliant blue eyes. She had never seen Jess this upset, but the intensity of his emotion didn't scare her in the slightest. As always, it thrilled and excited her, proved to her that he cared enough to get angry. Throughout the entire eight years of their marriage, Doug had rarely been moved to even raise his voice. After those idyllic first few months, nothing she'd said or done had ever mattered that much to him. Hotshot lawyer that he was, Doug had had much more important matters to concern himself with than the silly feelings of his naive little homebody of a wife.

Jess Hubbard, on the other hand, was making it quite clear that he would continue making demands until she told him exactly what she thought. He didn't care if she lost her temper with him or made an unladylike scene. He wouldn't tolerate anything less than an honest answer, even if he didn't like what that answer was.

Maybe it was in that moment that Terry discovered the truth, or maybe one small part of her consciousness had recognized what was happening to her while she and Jess had been making the wildest, most passionate love she'd ever experienced in her life, but suddenly she realized that she did need him in every way there was, including the most important way.

Heaven help her, but she loved the man! She was in love with Jesse Hubbard! For all the high blown promises she'd made to herself about listening to her head instead of her heart if she ever found herself involved with another man, she'd gone ahead and done the exact opposite. Where men were concerned, she was proof of the old maxim Once A Fool, Always The Fool.

Actually she was a much bigger fool this time around with Jess than she had been with Doug. At least back when she'd agreed to marry Doug, she'd been convinced that he was in love with her. Jess hadn't offered any such assurance, and she couldn't expect to receive one in the future, but had that stopped her from falling head over heels?

"No...no...no," she whispered miserably, and that litany of denial set off another explosive tirade.

"I swear, Teresa Louise Brubacker, I'm going to prove that you need me, even if I have to keep you out here all night long!" Jess ranted, his rugged features contorted in outrage as he let go of her arm, reached up with both hands, and grasped her tightly by her bare shoulders. "I'm going to love you every which way there is, and if that doesn't convince you that we need to get married right away, then I'll damned well start in on you all over again!"

Terry lifted her chin, desperate to retain even a small amount of her dignity since it was painfully obvious to her that this hateful man had taken everything else. He'd already stolen her heart and her pride. What more did he want? In her opinion, she'd provided quite enough proof of her vulnerability where his kind of lovemaking was concerned, so there was certainly no need for him to issue these lurid threats.

"It won't be necessary to place your brand on my forehead, cowboy," she informed him tartly. "I'm convinced, all right? You've convinced me."

Although his steely grasp on her shoulders didn't lessen any, Jess lost the urge to shake her, and his furious expression was replaced by a confused frown. "You're convinced of what?"

Okay, Terry thought to herself, the man was on his knees in front of her, but he certainly hadn't issued a romantic proposal, so she wasn't going to respond like the lovesick female she actually was. With a long, drawn-out sigh of resignation, she said, "Since we're well and truly stuck with each other for many more years to come, getting married is the practical thing to do."

Considering the colossal effort it had taken him to get her acceptance of his proposal, Jess should have been highly elated, but he wasn't. "You make it sound like you've just agreed to show up at your own funeral," he choked out indignantly.

"If you don't let me get dressed pretty darned soon, I'm going to freeze to death, and that's exactly where I will end up," Terry informed him acidly, then pointing to the gooseflesh that also covered his naked arms, she observed, "Of course, maybe we should stay right here until we turn to ice. In the long run, we might be much happier sharing a casket than a bed."

"You know damned well that I make you extremely happy in bed!"

Terry threw her arms up in exasperation, her gaze withering. "Will you *please* stop belaboring that point? Sexually, you make me very happy. Okay? Extremely happy...overwhelmingly happy...so happy it boggles my mind!''

He should've realized what kind of reaction his behavior would provoke out of her, Jess told himself a few minutes later as he struggled to pull on his jeans. He shouldn't have pushed her so hard, hammered her over the head with the fact that he had the power to control her body. Terry wasn't the type of woman a man should force into doing anything, let alone something as important as marriage, even if it was the best solution for her and everybody else concerned.

He'd known all along that she was the hearts and flowers type, harbored romantic fantasies about moonlight and roses. He'd been wise enough to provide the moonlight, and romantic enough to make love to her beneath a starlit sky, but afterward, when she didn't immediately leap at the chance to marry him, he'd lost patience and ruined everything. Eventually he'd managed to browbeat her into submission, but now he feared that he could very well spend the rest of his days paying for it.

Maybe not in bed, he decided. Terry would continue to surrender willingly to him there, but Jess couldn't even feel good about that. By "belaboring" that particular point, he'd made himself look like one of those wimps who were so insecure about their sexual performance that they forced their lovers to reassure them with repeated verbal confirmation. The prospect that Terry saw him as one of those unaspiring weaklings was so humiliating, Jess suspected that he might be doomed by a self-fulfilling prophesy.

The following Saturday morning, when he donned his navy blue suit and stood up before the town judge, he was still worried about that possibility. Terry had agreed to marry him, but every night since then he'd been plagued by bad dreams depicting his humiliating failure to consummate their marriage. The dreams had tormented him so much that he'd barely said two words to his prospective bride for an entire week.

Terry obviously wasn't suffering from similar qualms. Besides looking absolutely fantastic in her pink, flowery silk dress and matching hat, her expression was annoyingly serene. Unlike him, she didn't seem one bit worried about their uncertain future together, but by the end of the marriage ceremony, wherein he'd promised to love, honor, and cherish her until death, Jess felt very close to panic. Somehow, even though his hands were shaking badly, he managed to shove the wedding ring on Terry's finger, and he was able to speak his I do's at the appropriate moment, but when he heard the magistrate announce that he and Terry were joined together by bonds that no man should put asunder, his knees buckled.

Although she was feeling slightly dazed herself, Terry didn't completely lose her balance when Jess staggered heavily against her. It took some effort, but she was able to keep him upright for the few seconds it took for Sam to step forward and help her hold him. Together they managed to guide Jess over to one of the judge's black leather chairs, and while Sam went out into the hallway to fetch a glass of water, Terry made sure that her less than enthusiastic new husband didn't lift his head up from between his knees.

After a minute she heard him muttering under his breath, and her lips started twitching. For all his fine talk about thinking the matter through, applying irrefutable male logic to every aspect of their situation, the silly man was not only having trouble dealing with the fact that he was now a husband but also the legal stepfather of two small boys. For some strange reason it had just dawned on Jess that both of these roles were for life.

Considering the way he'd coerced her into marrying him and highly resenting the fact that he'd all but ignored her every day since then, Terry wasn't feeling the least bit charitable when she leaned down and whispered in his ear, "You volunteered for this job, remember? Nobody held a shotgun to your head."

Jess turned his face up to cast a baleful eye at her, but the movement made him even more nauseous and he promptly returned his attention to the floor. "Well, you can go right ahead and shoot me now," he suggested miserably and Terry giggled.

"Being sick's not funny, Mom," Chad scolded. None too happy at being forced to wear a suit and certain that Jess felt the same, he jerked on his starchy white collar and declared, "Maybe his tie is too tight just like mine. Do you feel like choking, Jess?"

Chad didn't appear to require an answer to that question, but his younger brother went down on his haunches so he could peer up at Jess's ashen face. "Are you going to throw up on the carpet?" Chuck inquired curiously.

Jess mumbled something that apparently satisfied the little boy for he didn't protest when his red-faced mother reached down and yanked him back to his feet. "The bride is usually the one who faints," Judge Harold Riley declared jovially, a comment which inspired more than a mumble from the fallen groom.

Jess reared up in his chair, pushing Terry's restraining hands off his back as he half shouted, "I did not faint, dammit! It's so blasted hot in here, I'm just feeling a little dizzy."

"The bigger they are, the harder they fall," Sam decreed with a knowing laugh as he reentered the judge's air-conditioned chambers. "Here, son, maybe you'll feel better once you've had a drink."

"I'm feeling just fine," Jess snarled, but he snatched the glass out of Sam's hand and gulped down the water. Afterward he tried standing up, and when he only experienced a slight dizziness, he grabbed Terry's arm and growled, "Let's sign the necessary papers so we can get the hell out of this place. I've got over two hundred head of cattle to inoculate this afternoon."

Terry could understand and even sympathize with Jess's embarrassment. He was a proud man, used to handling every situation with total ease, but his manhandling of her made her angry, and she refused to let him get away with that last insulting comment. Obviously he considered their wedding an annoying glitch in his busy schedule, but he didn't have to utterly humiliate her in front of the judge.

"Oooooh! Isn't he just the most romantic man?" she asked the shocked official in such a saccharine tone that even Jess grimaced. "And so marvelously dedicated to his work?"

Fifteen minutes later the marriage license was signed and they were all back in the car. Unfortunately Jess still felt a bit woozy, which meant that he had to sit next to Terry on the front seat and leave the driving to Sam. The next thing he knew, the car was pulling off the highway into a tree-lined parking lot and his new grandfather-in-law was informing him that his wedding present to the newlyweds was a night at the only motel within a fifty-mile radius, the Twin Pines.

"I called the vet and told him not to come out until after noon tomorrow," Sam stated smoothly as he switched off the engine. "The boys and I figured that every bride deserves some kind of a honeymoon, even if it is for only one night. Chad and Chuck even packed a suitcase for you two, and I've got a feeling you'll find a nice surprise inside once you open it up."

"We made you a wedding present," Chad announced.

"And nobody helped us," Chuck declared proudly.

"I can't wait to see what it is," Terry told them, then followed Jess's gaze to the words outlined in blue neon lights on the motel sign.

Jess waited for Terry to finish reading the sign, supremely confident that she wouldn't step one foot in a place that advertised cheap hourly rates and vibrating beds. "Thanks, Sam," he said, but before he could make their excuses, Terry interrupted him.

"How very thoughtful of you, Grandpa, and we gratefully accept."

Jess practically swallowed his Adam's apple. "We do?"

"We do," Terry confirmed, and to make sure Jess didn't put up any further argument, she slid one hand under his elbow and jabbed him meaningfully in the ribs. "And thank you, boys, for going to the trouble of packing a suitcase and making us a wedding present. You and Grandpa have made this into a very special occasion for us, and we really appreciate it, don't we, Jess?"

Another sneaky elbow to the midsection guaranteed the required response. "You bet, fellas," Jess agreed weakly. "This is great . . . just great."

Ordinarily, being alone with a sexy woman in a raunchy motel room would have given Jess a few X-rated ideas, but Terry wasn't just any woman. She was his wife and the future mother of his children. A decent man wouldn't be caught dead in such a place with his wife, and he certainly wouldn't insult her by contending that she might enjoy the sensual delights that could be shared by two people on a water bed. A decent man wouldn't be curious about the panel of buttons he saw on the cheap, black plastic headboard, wouldn't even wonder what a little artificial vibration might do to heighten certain erotic sensations.

"I'm sorry, Terry, but this dump is no place for a honeymoon!" he burst out desperately. "A bride deserves better on her wedding night, much better."

Terry picked up the small suitcase Jess had set down near the door and started off in the direction of the bathroom. "Maybe so," she agreed briskly. "But beggars can't be choosers."

Jess stared morosely at the closed bathroom door, feeling like a first-class jerk. He'd been so wrapped up in his own feelings lately that he hadn't even considered Terry's. This was her wedding day, a day that should have been one of the happiest in her life, but he'd done absolutely nothing to insure her happiness. He'd suffered through the ten-minute ceremony then keeled over as if sickened by the thought of being shackled to her for the rest of his life. To make matter worse, he hadn't even arranged for a proper honeymoon for her. As soon as he was able, he'd hustled his beautiful bride right back out to the car so he could race out to the ranch and insure that a bunch of mangy heifers got their necessary inoculations.

"You really do deserve to be shot." Jess muttered to himself as he flung himself down on the room's one and only chair, a flimsy piece of furniture with uneven legs and imitation velvet cushions. "Purple velour curtains, that's what you've given your wife, Hubbard. Jeezus, Mary, and Martha! Purple curtains, a gold tassled lamp, and cheap, red satin sheets!"

Ten

Terry deserved an abject apology, Jess decided grimly as he jerked on his tie and undid the top two buttons on his white shirt. And she was going to get it, he vowed, the instant she came back out of the bathroom. Perhaps if he explained that his poorly equipped male system had suffered from some extremely painful shocks in recent days, not the least of which was the realization that he didn't know the first thing about being a good husband or father, she'd take pity on him. Maybe if he came right out and admitted to her that he'd spent the last week running away from the truth, she'd even find it in her heart to forgive him for his total lack of sensitivity.

As the minutes ticked by, he rehearsed the speech he was going to say to her over and over again in his mind, but when the door to the bathroom finally re-opened and his bride walked back into the room, Jess was struck dumb. Her hat was gone and so was her pretty pink dress, and in their place was a shimmering, midnight blue nightgown made out of some translucent fabric that allowed him to see every luscious curve of her body.

"What do you think of this little number?" Terry inquired, as she stepped in front of him and whirled around in a circle, providing him with a tantalizing glimpse of her long, silky legs. "Not exactly something you'd expect a seventy-five-year-old man to pick out for his granddaughter, is it?"

"Sam bought you that!"

Terry nodded, then went back into the bathroom and returned with a small package wrapped in yellow construction paper and decorated with happy faces. "Once I discovered Sam's surprise, I didn't have the nerve to open this. How about if you do the honors?"

She dropped the package onto Jess's lap, but he was so entranced by the tiny, blue satin ribbons that held the two sides of her flimsy bodice together that he hadn't heard a single thing she'd said, and Terry was forced to repeat herself. "C'mon, Jess, open it. I can't wait to see Chad and Chuck's idea of the perfect wedding present."

For the second time in the course of one day, Jess found that his hands were shaking, but after a bit of fumbling, he finally managed to unwrap the package and pull off the top of the box. He stared down at the contents for a long time, then mumbled in a strangled tone, "I think it's supposed to be a family portrait."

Smiling with pleasure, Terry knelt down beside his chair, unaware of Jess's sharp intake of breath as she rested one arm casually on his upper thigh and reached into the box to lift out the notched sticks of white pine that had been glued into an imperfect square. "This is a pretty good frame," she judged proudly, but immediately fell silent when she viewed the picture her sons had drawn with their color crayons.

Grandpa Sam was easily recognizable because of his scribbly gray beard, and the two, much shorter stick figures standing beside him had to be Chad and Chuck. It was obvious that the tall figure in the cowboy hat was supposed to be Jess, and the only person depicted with a dress had to be Terry. All five people in the drawing were smiling, but it wasn't their obvious happiness that fostered the lump in Jess's throat or the catch in Terry's voice. "Do you think that's a . . . baby girl or a . . . baby boy?"

Jess had to clear his throat before he could trust his voice enough to speak. "I'd say it's a girl. No son of mine would be wearing pink."

Terry nodded, unable to take her eyes off the tiny body clasped in her stick-figured arms. "A little girl," she murmured dreamily.

Jess studied her enraptured expression, and his heart began thudding so hard it was almost painful. "You wouldn't mind having another baby? My baby?"

Hearing the note of incredulity in his voice, Terry lifted her chin, her lips turned up slightly at the corners as she assured him. "No, I wouldn't mind at all, and after two boys, I especially like the thought of having a daughter. Would you mind if we had a girl?''

''No,'' Jess declared gruffly as a vivid picture formed in his mind, a picture of Terry, her belly swollen with his child. ''I wouldn't mind that at all.''

''Good,'' Terry replied firmly. ''Because I'm not taking anything to prevent getting pregnant.''

Jess grinned at the militant set of her chin. ''You won't get any argument about that from me. I'm glad you feel that way.''

''You are?''

Jess nodded. ''Very glad, because I didn't use any protection the other night so there's already a chance that you could be pregnant.''

''So there is,'' Terry declared wonderingly, as if that possibility had never dawned on her before, which it hadn't. All she'd been capable of thinking about that night under the stars was the intense pleasure she'd felt in his arms, the incredible delight she'd experienced at being one with him.

Then something else occurred to her and she frowned. ''You planned to make love to me that night. Was it also your intention to make me pregnant?''

Jess knew what she was thinking and also realized that he'd given her ample reason to doubt his motives. From her point of view, his efforts to convince her to marry him must have looked extremely cold and calculating. The suspicion in her voice made it clear that she wouldn't even put it past him to get her pregnant if that would insure her consent. But then Terry didn't know what he'd only just discovered. When it came to his feelings for her, cold-blooded logic just didn't apply, and his calculations concerning the necessity of their marriage had all been based on the wrong premise.

"I deserve that," he acknowledged ruefully. "But believe me, when I made love to you, Terry, that's all I was thinking about. The reality of finally having you naked in my arms was enough to knock every other rational thought out of my head. I hate to admit this, but around you I seem to go a little bit crazy. Birth control was the last thing on my mind."

It wasn't exactly a declaration of love, but it was better than nothing and Terry smiled. Someday, if she were very patient, maybe she would hear the words she so desperately wanted to hear, but for now, she would just have to be content with what he was willing to offer, and that offer wasn't bad. At least Jess admitted to wanting her so badly that he lost control, and she had great faith that his wanting would eventually turn to loving. In the meantime she had more than enough love in her heart for both of them.

"I'm very familiar with that feeling," she admitted honestly.

Jess took hold of her hands, then stood up, drawing her up to face him. "Are you?" he inquired tautly, an urgency in his voice that Terry had never heard before. "Do I make you feel a little crazy?"

"Definitely," Terry murmured, deliberately holding his gaze as she lifted her hands to her bodice and began untying the narrow satin ribbons. "Especially times like now when I want you so very badly."

No longer afraid of admitting her passionate hunger for him, a hunger she knew would never abate, she pulled the ends of the last bow, and the midnight blue silk fell away from her body, sliding down her hips to the floor.

"Terry..."

She liked her husband's rapt expression, savored the appreciation that darkened and narrowed his eyes and quickened his breathing as he looked down at her. She knew that her breasts were high and full and firm, and she displayed them brazenly, her heart throbbing wildly in her chest. "Very, very badly," she insisted softly.

There was something Jess had intended to tell her, needed to tell her before he completely lost his head, but he couldn't quite remember what that something was as Terry stepped closer to him. Slowly she unbuttoned his shirt while he watched her, a disbelieving expression on his face as she separated the material and her hands began to explore his naked chest. Then her arms slid around his waist as she was pressing her firm breasts against him, and he stopped thinking altogether.

"Lord," he groaned, his hands clasped over her shoulders as he moved her abrasively against him so that he could feel her silky firm flesh and aroused peaks brushing eagerly against him. She was so warm, so incredibly giving, and after the lousy way he'd treated her all week, he didn't deserve such generosity, but he accepted it. When he felt her fingers on his belt, he practically stopped breathing, and after that, his paralyzed body gave him no choice but to accept anything and everything she chose to do with him.

His heart ran wild when her hands found him, blatantly caressed him in the place she'd never touched before, and he almost went to his knees with the force of the passion she aroused. No matter how valiantly he tried, he couldn't control his reactions to her, and for once Jess didn't try. Instead of feeling vulnerable beneath her power, he felt as if he could conquer the world.

Terry felt his hunger for her and moved even closer, letting her thighs touch his, drowning in the remembered pleasure of flesh against burning flesh. She was on fire for him, just as she had been the first time they'd made love. She arched backward so that she could see his face, hoping to find the same desperate longing on his features that she was feeling.

"Do you want me as much as I want you?" she whispered.

"I want you more," he said, his voice harsh and almost unrecognizable. "And I want you now!"

He bent and lifted her, pressing his mouth hungrily against one full, perfect breast and glorying in her passionate response.

Terry moaned sharply, opening her eyes as he lifted his head. She shuddered in his hard embrace, feeling his body absorb the shock of his steps as he carried her to the bed, ripped away the purple velvet spread, and laid her down upon the cool, satin sheets. He stretched out on his side next to her, a low laugh rumbling in his chest as the water-filled mattress undulated beneath them, tossing their bodies gently against each other, then farther away.

"Kinky," he murmured, but took shocking advantage of the languid movement of the bed, his lips nuzzling her neck, then whispering across the curve of one breast and over her shoulder, receding with the increasingly gentle motion of the waves. His hands swiftly followed his lips, and he used them to drive her wild as he moved deliberately to set off another swell of sensual rocking. As the mattress heaved up and down, back and forth, he slid down the length of her body, then kissed his way back up.

His tongue stroked the sensitive skin of her inner thighs, and his hands caressed her, his fingers sliding upward to ease inside her. With the slight downward motion of his knee, he provoked another set of gentle undulations, and Terry gasped at the shocks of pleasure that shot through her. When Jess added his own stroking rhythm to the tormenting motion of the bed, the throbbing inside her became so insistent that a moan was forced from her throat.

She felt him shudder, then move, pushing her thighs wide apart as he came down over her. He eased into her slowly, gently, but then he stopped and reached an arm over her shoulder. "Jess?" Terry questioned, but when she felt the quivering vibrations, she realized that he'd pressed one of the buttons on the overhead panel. "Oh!" she gasped as she felt the tiny pulsations build higher and higher, until she could feel them deep inside her womb.

Jess moved again, just a bit, drawing back then pushing forward, feeling her muscles tighten and convulse around him as she fell over the edge. He closed his eyes, absorbing her pleasure into himself, savoring the intensity of her climax before seeking his own satisfaction. He wanted her with him when he found his release, but not just in body. He wanted all of her and that wanting just seemed to get more and more powerful, and he now accepted that, silently pledged to hold true to the vows he'd spoken to her before the judge.

When she quieted, his fingers stroked over her stomach and found her, and he began his caressing rhythm again, only this time he filled her completely. Terry began to move with him, arched her hips to meet each wild thrust. She could feel the agony of tension gripping every muscle in his body and knew that she had the power to release that tension. She wrapped her legs around his hips, taking him deeper and deeper inside her as the spiraling tension built to a whirlwind that hurled them both toward ecstasy and over-whelming fulfillment.

For several minutes Jess didn't have the strength to roll away from her, would have been happy to stay right where he was forever, but he needed to know that Terry shared his feelings. He moved to his side then, propped his head up with one elbow, and tried to look casual as he smiled down at the woman lying beside him...his woman! "This is what we'll have for the next forty or fifty years," he drawled. "I can live with that. How about you?"

Terry smiled up at him, but her dark eyes shimmered with incredible sadness. "I can live with that," she whispered, but Jess could hear the strain in her voice.

Suddenly his heart felt like lead in his chest. "But that thought doesn't make you happy?"

Terry wished that he'd never asked her such a pointed question, knew that to answer him honestly would be a huge mistake, but after making love to him, she couldn't lie about her feelings. "I'm afraid not, Jess," she murmured reluctantly, unable to prevent the tears that moistened her eyes. "I'm sorry...but until you love me as much as I love you, I can't be completely happy. I agreed to settle for less when I married you, but I won't be content with that agreement for the next forty years. I...I can't be."

"You actually mean that?" he inquired unsteadily, searching her dark eyes with his own. "You love me?"

Terry tried to look away, but Jess brought his hand to her chin, forcing her to meet his gaze. "I'm sorry," she whispered, but couldn't prevent a trace of bitterness from creeping into her tone as she said. "I know you've worked everything out to your satisfaction and didn't figure that kind of complication into our nice, practical arrangement, but I can't help how I feel."

His eyes blazed with some unrecognizable emotion, but his features looked like they'd been carved out of granite, and Terry misread his expression. "You don't have to look so grim," she advised tartly. "Loving you is my problem, not yours!"

"Not true," Jess contradicted her as he sat up straight in the bed. "Loving me is my problem, too, since at the moment, I don't even like me."

Terry sat up, too, her brows knit in confusion as she rested her stiff shoulders back against the headboard. "Huh?"

"What's to like?" Jess demanded. "Only a real jerk would treat the woman he loves the way I've treated you. For the past week I've acted like you had the bubonic plague or something, but I really proved what a lowlife I am by getting sick at our wedding, then trying to salvage my wounded pride by telling the judge that I had more interest in a bunch of ugly cows than my beautiful bride. And then, did I stop there? Oh no, fool that I am, I allowed us to end up in a scuzzy place like this because I was far too overwhelmed by the knowledge that I loved you to think about arranging for a decent honeymoon."

Terry had stopped breathing long before he finished his astounding speech, and her heart didn't start again for several moments after he'd finished berating himself. "Would you..." She had to clear her throat before she could get the words out. "Would you kindly repeat that?"

Jess looked shocked. "All of it?"

Terry shook her head, her gaze locked on his face as if she couldn't quite believe the adoration she saw in his blue eyes. "Just the first part," she replied, waving one hand in an urgent, circular motion. "The part about me being the woman you love."

He smiled sheepishly at her, then bent down and kissed her mouth tenderly. "If you don't mind, I'd rather demonstrate that part."

Terry did mind. She minded very much, and before his touch made her forget how much she minded, she scooted up and over the boxy frame of the bed. Jess smiled at the delightful sight of her beautifully naked body standing before him, and a warm rush of heat washed over him, but Terry forced herself not to respond to the heat in his eyes. With a warning frown, she grabbed up the tacky purple velour spread and wrapped herself up in it.

"From the first day we met, Jess Hubbard, you taunted and provoked me into speaking my mind, but now it's your turn. I want a full explanation, and you're not touching me again until I get it."

Jess gave her his most appealing smile. "Do we have to do this right now, honey? We've only got this room for twenty-four hours, and once we go home, we won't have this kind of privacy. Come on, sweetheart, do you really want to stand around talking when we could be making love?"

"To tell you the truth, lambykins," Terry cooed. "I'm prepared to stand here until hell freezes over."

Jess sighed in resignation, accepting that she wouldn't allow him to put her off any longer even if the words he needed to say proved very difficult to come. "This has been the toughest week I've ever suffered through in my life," he complained.

"If you don't start talking, it's going to get a lot tougher."

"Okay, okay," Jess admitted defeat, then patted the sheets next to him and promised, "I'll be good."

Although it was probably not a very wise move on her part, Terry gave him the benefit of the doubt and climbed back into bed, pulling the top sheet up over them both as they leaned back against the headboard. "Just when exactly did you discover that you loved me? Details, Mr. Hubbard," she declared, dark eyes gleaming with feminine relish. "I want to hear all the romantic details."

Jess rolled his eyes but thought better of disobeying even if that word hadn't been included in his part of the marriage ceremony. "As you may recall, we made love for the first time last Friday night and it was all downhill for me from there," he admitted resentfully. "On Saturday I decided that I not only wanted your body, but that I kind of liked you even if you were a bossy sort."

Terry made a horrid face that would've made her two sons proud. "Bossy! You think *I'm* bossy?"

Jess stared pointedly down his nose at her, and Terry nodded. "Right," she conceded. "You kind of liked the bossy woman you'd proposed to. Then what happened?"

"By Sunday I'd concluded that marriage to you was a sound business decision and for the good of the Triple L, I was willing to make the supreme sacrifice."

"Sacrif—!"

Jess lowered his sharply arched brow and continued. "On Monday I was back to the lust angle. Lust was a good enough reason for any man to get married, especially when the woman I lusted after was also a great cook."

He paused and looked over at her, waiting for her indignant outburst, but Terry had one hand clamped firmly over her mouth. "The raging hormone issue tided me over until Wednesday, but then I started worrying that I wasn't being very fair to you. Knowing that lust is usually a temporary condition, I had to come up with a more acceptable reason for forcing you into a permanent relationship, and I decided that you needed me to look after you. Once we were married, it would be my duty to take care of you and the boys, and that would make everything all fair and square. I'd get the use of your body, not to mention all the baking powder biscuits I could eat, and you'd get my protection.''

The look in his wife's eyes was extremely daunting, but she didn't lower her hand, and Jess blundered on, figuring that he couldn't do any more damage to himself than he'd already done thus far. ''Something still didn't feel right to me by today, but after the ruthless way I'd gone about convincing you to marry me, I didn't dare back out of our deal. Then I stood up before the judge, and the truth hit me squarely between the eyes.''

Terry mumbled something between her fingers, but when Jess looked over suspiciously at her, she gave him an encouraging toss of her head. ''Damnation, if I weren't in love with you,'' he declared in a disbelieving tone, as if even now he was having trouble digesting that amazing fact. ''Today I found out that I wasn't marrying you to ensure the future of the ranch or for the chance to be a good father to two fine boys. Nor for any of the other stupid reasons I'd previously considered, not even my insatiable lust for your baking powder biscuits.''

After a long pause he burst out harshly, ''You're the woman I've been searching for my whole life, the missing part of my soul that I'd never expected to find and refused to recognize even when I did.''

Out of the corner of his eye, Jess saw Terry take her hand away from her mouth. Then she was swinging it in his direction, and he winced, anticipating the sting of her open palm against his cheek. Instead of delivering a slap, however, Terry tailed her fingers tenderly along the side of his face. "Like Grandpa Sam always says, The Bigger They Are, The Harder They Fall."

"You're not mad at me?" Jess demanded incredulously. "You understand why I've been behaving like such an unfeeling jerk all week?"

"Your wife is an extremely understanding woman," Terry replied tartly, but all the love in her heart was shining in her eyes. "Especially since you redeemed yourself so sweetly there at the end. Telling me that I'm the woman you've been searching for all your life, the missing part of your soul, makes up for all the other less than romantic things you said."

"From now on, Mrs. Hubbard, I intend to be the most romantic man in the world. It's going to be hearts and flowers for you, everyday for the rest of your life. Moonlight and roses, the whole ball of wax," Jess vowed, then realized how hard it was going to be for him to live up to that promise and growled fiercely, "Even if it kills me."

Terry laughed. "Which it would in a couple of days, and I'd like to spend a bit more time with you before you make me a widow. Even if you aren't the most romantic man in the world, I still love you and I'd be willing to settle for similar declarations on your part.

Like…maybe…every other day or so? Whenever you happen to think about it?''

Jess considered her generous proposal for a moment, loving her so damned much that he felt like bursting. "I think I can do even better than that."

"You can?"

"You betcha."

Reaching up, he pulled the gold chain up over his head then down over hers, his touch gentle as he settled his lucky gold piece between her full breasts. While he admired how it looked in that spot, he told Terry the story of his Great-Great-Grandmother Cornelia and the bushwhacker, then explained how his Great-Aunt Ophelia had passed the coin on to him.

"No wonder you've never taken it off," Terry said when he finished speaking, deeply touched that he'd presented his fondest personal possession to her. "I'll cherish it, Jess. Always."

"Just as I'll always cherish you," Jess murmured, leaning over to drop a tender kiss on her lips. "I used that coin for luck and to remind me of my home and my family, but with you around, I don't need anything else to remind me. Maybe it took me awhile to get around to accepting the facts, but I already know them by heart. You're my luck, Mrs. Hubbard, my home and my family. This drifter has finally found the place where he's going to be blissfully content until the end of his born days, and that place is wherever you are."

"And I'm right here, Jess," Terry whispered fervently, reaching out with both arms and pulling him down on top of her. "And I plan to stay here until the cows come home."

Just before his lips claimed hers, Jess inquired blankly, "What cows?"

*   *   *   *   *

IT'S A CELEBRATION OF MOTHERHOOD!

Following the success of BIRDS, BEES and BABIES, we are proud to announce our second collection of Mother's Day stories.

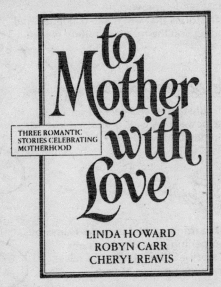

to
Mother
with
Love

THREE ROMANTIC
STORIES CELEBRATING
MOTHERHOOD

LINDA HOWARD
ROBYN CARR
CHERYL REAVIS

Three stories in one volume, all by award-winning authors—stories especially selected to reflect the love all families share.

Available in May, TO MOTHER WITH LOVE is a perfect gift for yourself or a loved one to celebrate the joy of motherhood.

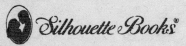

Silhouette Books®

ML-1

FOUR UNIQUE SERIES
FOR EVERY WOMAN YOU ARE...

Silhouette Romance®

Love, at its most tender, provocative, emotional... in stories that will make you laugh and cry while bringing you the magic of falling in love.

6 titles per month

Silhouette Special Edition®

Sophisticated, substantial and packed with emotion, these powerful novels of life and love will capture your imagination and steal your heart.

6 titles per month

SILHOUETTE Desire®

Open the door to romance and passion. Humorous, emotional, compelling—yet always a believable and sensuous story—Silhouette Desire never fails to deliver on the promise of love.

6 titles per month

SILHOUETTE·INTIMATE·MOMENTS®

Enter a world of excitement, of romance heightened by suspense, adventure and the passions every woman dreams of. Let us sweep you away.

4 titles per month

Take 4 bestselling love stories FREE

Plus get a FREE surprise gift!

Special Limited-time Offer

Silhouette Reader Service®

Mail to

In the U.S.
3010 Walden Avenue
P.O. Box 1867
Buffalo, N.Y. 14269-1867

In Canada
P.O. Box 609
Fort Erie, Ontario
L2A 5X3

YES! Please send me 4 free Silhouette Desire® novels and my free surprise gift. Then send me 6 brand-new novels every month, which I will receive months before they appear in bookstores. Bill me at the low price of $2.24* each—a savings of 51¢ apiece off cover prices. There are no shipping, handling or other hidden costs. I understand that accepting the books and gift places me under no obligation ever to buy any books. I can always return a shipment and cancel at any time. Even if I never buy another book from Silhouette, the 4 free books and the surprise gift are mine to keep forever.

*Offer slightly different in Canada—$2.24 per book plus 69¢ per shipment for delivery. Sales tax applicable in N.Y. Canadian residents add applicable federal and provincial taxes.

225 BPA JAZP (US)   326 BPA 8177 (CAN)

Name	(PLEASE PRINT)
Address	Apt. No.
City	State/Prov. Zip/Postal Code

This offer is limited to one order per household and not valid to present Silhouette Desire® subscribers. Terms and prices are subject to change.

DES-BPA1DR   © 1990 Harlequin Enterprises Limited

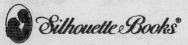